MISCHIEF

CHARLOTTE ARMSTRONG

Charlotte Armstrong was born in 1905 in Michigan USA. After getting a degree from Columbia University she worked at various jobs: taking classified advertisements for the *New York Times*, as a fashion reporter and as an office worker. She started writing at eight years of age, and eventually began contributing poems to the *New Yorker*, and writing plays. While her second play *Ring Around Elizabeth* was being produced on Broadway, she had her first mystery story *Lay On Macduff* published. She wrote more than 20 books during her life, several of which have been made into films. Combining a successful career as author and playwright, she lived in California with her husband and their three children. She died in 1969.

Already published in Pandora Women Crime Writers:

Green For Danger by Christianna Brand
Death of a Doll by Hilda Lawrence
Murder in Pastiche by Marion Mainwaring
Amateur City by Katherine V. Forrest
Bring The Monkey by Miles Franklin
Stoner McTavish by Sarah Dreher
The Port of London Murders by Josephine Bell
The Spinster's Secret by Anthony Gilbert (Lucy Malleson)

To be published in 1988:

Something Shady by Sarah Dreher
Fieldwork by Maureen Moore
Vanishing Act by Joy Magezis
The Hours Before Dawn by Celia Fremlin
Easy Prey by Josephine Bell
London Particular by Christianna Brand

These will be joined in the future with more novels by Josephine Bell, Ina Bouman, Pamela Branch, Christianna Brand, Celia Fremlin, Gladys Mitchell, Baroness Orczy and many other of the best women crime writers.

MISCHIEF

CHARLOTTE ARMSTRONG

London

First published in Great Britain by Peter Davies in 1951
This edition first published in Great Britain in 1988 by
Pandora Press (Routledge)
11 New Fetter Lane, London EC4P 4EE

Set in Linotron Sabon 10/11½pt
by Input Typesetting Ltd, London, SW19 8DR
and printed in Great Britain
by Cox & Wyman Ltd, Reading

British Library Cataloging in Publication Data
Armstrong, Charlotte
Mischief.—(Pandora women crime
writers).
I. Title
813'.52 [F]   PS3501.R566

ISBN 0–86358–272–9

Pandora Women Crime Writers

Series Editors: Rosalind Coward and Linda Semple

In introducing the *Pandora Women Crime Writers* series we have two aims: to reprint the best of women crime writers who have disappeared from print and to introduce a new generation of women crime writers to all devotees of the genre. We also hope to seduce new readers to the pleasures of detective fiction.

Women have used the tradition of crime writing inventively since the end of the last century. Indeed, in many periods women have dominated crime writing, as in the so-called Golden Age of detective fiction, usually defined as between the first novel of Agatha Christie and the last of Dorothy L. Sayers. Often the most popular novels of the day, and those thought to be the best in the genre, were written by women. But as in so many areas of women's writing, many of these have been allowed to go out of print. Few people know the names of Josephine Bell, Pamela Branch, Hilda Lawrence, Marion Mainwaring or Anthony Gilbert (whose real name was Lucy Malleson). Their novels are just as good and entertaining as when they were first written.

Women's importance in the field of crime writing is just as important today. P. D. James, Ruth Rendell and Patricia Highsmith have all ensured that crime writing is treated seriously. Not so well known, but equally flourishing is a new branch of feminist crime writing. We plan to introduce many new writers from this area, from England and other countries.

The integration of reprints and the new feminist novels is sometimes uneasy. Some writers do make snobbish, even racist remarks. However, it is a popular misconception that all earlier novels are always snobbish and racist. Many of our chosen and favourite authors managed to avoid, sometimes deliberately, the prevailing views. Others are more rooted in the ideologies of their time and when their remarks jar, it does serve to remind us that any novel must be understood by reference to the historical context in which it was written.

Linda Semple
Rosalind Coward

CHAPTER 1

Mr Peter O. Jones, editor and publisher of the Brennerton *Star-Gazette*, was standing in a bathroom in a hotel in New York City, scrubbing his nails. Through the open door his wife Ruth saw his naked neck stiffen, saw him fix his image with his eye, heard him declaim over the rush of running water, 'Ladies and gentlemen . . .' She winked at Bunny.

Ruth in her long petticoat was sitting at the dressing-table, having resolved to be as perfectly, as exquisitely groomed as ever a woman was in the world, this night. She was very gently powdering her thin bare shoulders. Every fair hair on her head was already in shining order. Her carefully reddened lips kept smiling, because she knew this long-drawn-out ritual, this polishing of every tooth and every toenail, was only to heighten the wonderful fun.

It was The Night. Ruth sighed, from a complexity of emotions.

What a formula, she thought, is a hotel room. Everything one needs. And every detail pursued with such heavy-handed comfort, such gloomy good taste, it becomes a formula for luxury. The twin beds, severely clean, austerely spread. The lamp and the telephone between. Dresser, dressing-table. Desk and desk chair (if the human unit needs to take his pen in hand). Bank of windows, on a court, with the big steam radiator across below them, metal-topped. Curtains in hotel-écru. Draperies in hotel-brocade. Easy chair in hotel-maroon. The standing lamp. The standing ashtray, that hideous useful thing. The vast empty closet. And the bath. The tiles. The big towels. The small soap. The very hot water.

Over this basic formula they had spread the froth of their preparations in that jolly disorder that a hotel room permits. Her rose-coloured evening dress swung with the hook of its hanger over the closet door. Peter's rummaged suitcase stood open on the luggage bench and his things were strewn on his bed. The dresser top was piled with stuff that at home would have been hidden in the drawers. Powder and ashes had spilled gloriously on the carpet. All the lights were blazing.

All the lights were blazing in Bunny's room too, the adjoining room that was exactly like this one, except that left was right and maroon was blue.

Peter turned the water off, reached for a towel, stood in the bathroom door in singlet and his dress trousers with his suspenders hanging down over his rump. Turning out his patent-leather toes, he bowed. 'Ladies and gentlemen . . .' He began to pantomime, clowning for Bunny. Ruth thought, fondly, How clever he is! She turned to watch what she loved to see, the smooth skin of Bunny's face ripple and twinkle as it always did before the giggle came out.

Bunny was nine. Her dark brows went up at the outside just like Peter's. In her blue woolly robe, Bunny hunched on the foot of Ruth's bed, her arms around her ankles, and one bunny-slipper stepping on the toe of the other. Her dark hair went smoothly back into the fat braids so often living and warm in Ruth's hands. Ruth's heart felt as if something squeezed it, quickly, and as quickly let it go.

Peter, with a fine-flung gesture, called down fire from heaven to be witness to his wordless passion, and bowed to make-believe applause. Bunny took her cue, let go her ankles, clapped once, lost her balance and toppled over giggling.

'You see!' said Peter, poking the blue bundle on the bed in a ticklish spot. 'Going to mow 'em down!'

'Peter,' said Ruth in fright and curiosity, 'do you know what you're going to say?'

'Well, I know what I'm going to *do*. I'm going to rise up and take a good grip on the rug with my toes and open my mouth. Oh, sure, I know what I'm going to say, in a way. I don't know how I'm going to put it, if that's what you mean.'

'Oh, Peter!' She sucked in breath. She didn't understand how anyone could do such a thing as make a speech. Something made her heart jump at the mere thought of it.

'Don't get me wrong,' said Peter. 'I'm terrified.' She knew he was. She knew he'd make the speech, nevertheless, and do it well. She knew, too, that her own tense partisanship was helpful to him, and even her fright was a channel that drew off some of his.

' . . . time is it, honey?'

'Quarter after six.' Their eyes met, briefly. Hers with a flick of worry. His with that quick dark reassurance.

He picked his dress shirt with the studs all in place off his bed. 'Which one of you two dames wants to button me up?'

'Me!' squealed Bunny. So Peter sat on the hard rim of the foot-board. 'Daddy, why does your shirt pretend it buttons in the front when it buttons in the back?'

'Civilization. Tradition in the front. Business in the back. How you doing?'

'O.K.,' said Bunny with a puff of effort. She never questioned Peter's polysyllables.

Business, thought Ruth darkly. 'Peter,' she said, 'I hope you know what I think of your sister Betty!'

'I couldn't print it,' he answered promptly.

'Business,' said Ruth as darkly as she felt. 'Her and her business appointment! On a Saturday night! *I* think she's got a heavy date.'

'Can't tell,' said Peter lightly, cautiously.

'I don't see *how* she could break her date with us! Do you? Really?'

Ruth heard again Betty's high and somewhat affected voice on the phone. ' . . . Terribly sorry, darling. Of course, if you simply can't get anyone, I'll cut this thing and I *will* come. . . . But I thought perhaps, if you *could* . . . ?' and Ruth stiffened once more with that shock and the anger.

Important! What kind of business appointment could be so important for Betty Jones — the silly little chit! Here in New York six months, with her job that paid what? fifty dollars a week? What on earth could Betty Jones do on a Saturday night that could be Important Business?

For years now Ruth had resented, but been unable to combat, her sister-in-law's manner that assumed, so ignorantly and unjustly, that Ruth was done for. Ruth's goose was cooked. Oh, Ruth was buried with the rank and file, and the drab stones all said Housewife, that drab and piteous label. There was no use. One could only wait and someday . . .

'We'll try, Betty,' Ruth had said, very coldly, and hung up and turned an anguished face to Peter. What if she had to plead and beg? Or not go to the ball?

But Peter had fixed it. By some hocus-pocus, he had fared forth into the halls and passages of the hotel, and he had fixed it. And Ruth had called Betty back and said, coolly, 'Don't bother . . .'

'But how could she welsh like that,' murmured Ruth, 'when she knows . . .'

'Hold still, Daddy.'

'Excuse it, pet. Look, Ruthie. Sis takes herself awful hard as the career girl. You know that. Someday . . .' Their eyes met and the gleam in Peter's was satisfactory. 'Besides,' he went on, 'I don't suppose she thinks this convention amounts to much. Corn-fed gathering of country editors. Provincial, hm?'

'There you are!' said Ruth indignantly. 'There *you* sit, seeing *her* point of view. But can she see ours? Night of the banquet, and your speech, and it was all arranged weeks ago. What if we couldn't have gotten anybody?'

'She did say she'd come if she must. No use to be bitter.'

Ruth bit her lip.

'Don't fret, Cinderella,' grinned Peter. 'You shall go to the ball.'

Ruth blinked, because he was right . . . no use to be bitter. She kicked off her mules and bent to reach for her evening shoes, feeling the soft brush of her own hair on her bare shoulders. 'Oh, dem golden slippers . . .' whistled Peter, and Ruth saw Bunny's solemn eyes peek around his shoulder. For the audience, Ruth fell back into the rhythm. She arched her pretty feet and put them slowly, ceremoniously into her golden slippers.

'Someday,' said Peter, with his dark eyes glowing, 'do you know, girls, who's going to be putting on her golden slippers to go to the ball?'

'Bunny O. Jones,' said Ruth at once.

'And who's going to be sitting with their bedroom slippers on, watching her?'

'You and me,' Ruth said. Their eyes met, smiled. We'll grow old. It won't matter.

Bunny said, in a practical voice, 'Is my sitter coming pretty soon?'

Peter pinched the toes in the furry slippers. 'Pretty soon. And you're going to go to sleep in your room with two beds, one for each pigtail. And what are you going to do in the morning?'

'Telephone,' said Bunny.

'And say?'

'Room service.'

'And then?'

'This is Miss Bunny O. Jones. I want my breakfast, please.'

'In room?'

'Room 809.' Bunny flushed and started over again. 'This is Miss Bunny O. Jones in room 809. I want my breakfast, please. And if they don't know what I'm talking about, I'll say, My Daddy, Mr Peter O. Jones, ordered it last night.'

'And when the man knocks on the door?'

'I'll unlock the door and run quick back in my bed.'

'That's right. The key's in your door. And then they'll bring in the wagon.'

'Daddy, it isn't a real wagon.'

'No horses, I'll admit. A mere pushing type of wagon. And on it's going to be a whole bunch of silver dishes and your orange juice sitting in the biggest mess of cracked ice you ever saw, enough to make about four snowballs. And you'll eat your breakfast, putting on as much sugar and cream as you want, and after a while Daddy will groan and wake up.'

'And to-morrow's the day,' Ruth said, 'you're going to the magic eating store.'

'I don't bleeve it!' said Bunny, but her face was rippling.

'Oh, you don't, Miss Bunny O. Jones? Well, you'll see!'

They all three had the middle initial 'O'. Ruth's name had been Olsen, and Peter was delighted with the coincidence. People named Jones, claimed he, had to do something. Peter O. Jones, he always was. And Bunny ran it together so that more than once school records had used the apostrophe.

'Quite a lot like a zoo,' Peter was explaining. 'A whole bunch of little glass cages and in one there's a hot meat pie, and in another there's a big fat salad, and all you do is put in your nickels and presto chango.'

'But you have to have nickels,' said Bunny shrewdly.

'Well, yes,' said her daddy. 'In the olden days, a magic wand was the thing. Now, of course, it's nickels.' He grinned. He had begun the struggle with his collar.

'Peter,' said Ruth suddenly, 'do you believe in the elevator boy? Do you believe in his niece? Is she coming?'

'Certainly,' said Peter, with his brows winging. 'Why would he say so?'

'I don't know –' for Ruth, the room was rocking. The bright box it was had become dreamlike. And the city over which it hung was fabulous and all its denizens were phantoms.

'Said she'd be glad to,' Peter was saying. 'First, I spoke to that coloured woman, that awfully nice-looking woman, the one who was so friendly. But she's – uh – dated up. So this Eddie overheard us and he offered. Glad to earn the money, he said.'

'It takes nickels . . . ?' murmured Ruth.

'Papa's wand. Imagine, hon. This Eddie's been running the same elevator for fourteen years. You know which one he is, don't you?'

'I guess . . .'

'Lives up in the Bronx. No children, he told me. He'll tell you, at the drop of a hat. Speaks fondly of his wife. Must be a nice woman. This girl, now . . . they seem to have taken her in out of the goodness of their hearts since his brother died.' Peter sucked his cheek. 'Fourteen years, up and down. And he still runs that elevator as if his heart was in it to do it perfectly. I've seen 'em so blasé – make your hair curl. Wonder what he gets a week?'

Ruth sighed. Her momentary feeling that it was all myth was blown away. The little man who ran the elevator was real, of course . . . a human being, with a life, a wife, a budget . . . with brothers and sisters like everybody else and a niece to oblige. It was just like home, after all. You needed somebody. You asked around. It was just like asking the Johnstones who might say all their sitters were busy but they knew someone who knew somebody. You set up a kind of chain of inquiry and after a while it dredged up what you wanted. People were people and they passed the word and obliged each other and that was the way it went all over the world, truly.

'The niece comes from the Middle West someplace,' Peter was saying. 'Experienced, he says. I suppose a little extra means something in a setup like that.'

Ruth thought, all at once, that it was better to be paying someone, hiring someone, having a leverage of that power, than taking such a one as Betty's time for free. She smiled and reached out her hand.

'Oh boy,' said her husband, 'comes the twelve-dollar smell!'

'Twelve dollars and fifty cents, don't forget!' Ruth took the tiny stopper out, touched her shoulders with the precious stuff.

Peter bent over and sniffed violently. He said in her ear, 'Would a couple of symmetrical toothmarks look good?' She saw herself laughing, in the glass, and Peter's dark keen face against her yellow hair.

'. . . me smell,' demanded Bunny.

So Ruth crossed with her pretty petticoat swirling, turned the plump little paw, touched the back of it with the perfume. 'Dee-licious!' said Bunny, sniffing violently as her daddy had done.

Ruth looked down at the white clean part in the dark hair. All of a sudden, she saw their two connecting rooms, the two bright boxes on the inner rim of the doughnut of this eighth floor, suspended above the boiling city. And the rising noise surrounded them like smoke ... the honks, clangs, shouts and murmurs, the sound and fury ... and her heart was squeezed again. And she thought, We couldn't have left her two thousand miles away ... but we shouldn't have brought her ... but we couldn't have left her ...

The Hotel Majestic was neither large nor small, neither cheap nor costly. Not the last word, it wasn't dowdy, either. It was conservative. It tried to be smart about it, in a modest way. It took the middle road. Even the elevators, although they ran smoothly, did so with a modest speed.

Eddie Munro stopped for a light at the eighth floor. A young man got on, turned at once to face the door. They sank downward in silence.

Out of the corners of their eyes, they typed each other, quickly. Eddie saw the easy grace of a tall body, the arrogant carriage of the high head, the crew cut that was somehow arrogant, too. The sharp cut of the good-looking face, the long nose with the faint flare at the nostrils, the cool grey eyes, long-lashed, and almost beautiful in that hard-boned young face, but very cool and asking for nothing. A type. One of those young men who had come out of the late war with that drive, that cutting quality, as if they had shucked off human uncertainties and were aimed and hurtling toward something in the future about which they seemed very sure.

His name was Jed Towers. It was his last night in New York. He had a dinner date.

If he saw the little man out of the corner of his cool eye, it was just a little man, with his shoulders pulled back from his narrow chest in a frozen strut. With a grey face. With pale hair that never had any colour to lose, lying long and lank over the bald part. Pale eyes that blinked often, as if Eddie Munro was never quite sure of anything.

The car stopped smoothly at the main floor. Jed put his key on the desk without interrupting the long fluid strides that were taking him to the outside, to the city, to the evening.

Eddie ran a nervous glance around the quiet lobby. He said to the next boy, 'Gotta make a phone call. Watch it, will you?' He scuttled around a bend of wall with his nickel in his hand already.

'Marie?'

'Yeah, Eddie?' said his wife's placid voice.

'She leave?'

'She went, yeah, sure.'

'How long ago?'

'In plenty of time,' his wife said. Everything she said carried the overtone, Don't worry, Eddie.

'Take the subway?'

'Of course.'

'Listen, Marie, I think maybe I oughta stay around after I'm off. Folks might be late. Some kind of big shindig, the man said. O.K.?'

'O.K.'

'I think I oughta stay and bring her home, don't you?'

'Good idea, Eddie.'

'You do think the whole idea's a good idea, Marie? She can earn a little money? You know? Get started?'

'Sure it is, Eddie.'

'She – uh – liked the idea, didn't she?'

'Sure she did.'

'Well . . . uh . . .' He didn't want to let go of the wire, leading to Marie and her voice saying, Sure.

'Say, Eddie . . .'

'Yeah?'

I think maybe I'll go to the show. Miz Martin said she'd go with me.' Eddie squirmed in the booth, blinking rapidly. His wife's voice went on. 'That picture we didn't think we'd better take *her*? You know?'

'Yeah.'

'So I thought I'd go – got the chance.'

'Oh, well. Yeah. Sure.'

'Don't worry, Eddie,' Marie soothed. 'I'll be home long before you and Nell, probably.'

'Sure. Sure,' he said. He heard his wife's tiny sigh whispering on the wire. 'Go ahead,' he said vigorously. 'Have a good time.'

'It'll be O.K.,' she told him. (Don't worry, Eddie.)

He went around the wall to his car. His eyes searched toward the revolving door, across the depth of the lobby. He threw back his shoulders, trying to stand erect, to look as if he were perfectly sure.

In 807, Ruth slipped the rose-coloured frivolity off its hanger and expertly lowered it past her shining hair. Peter's strong fingers zipped her up the back. She made her curtsy to the audience.

'Something like a princess,' said Peter judiciously, 'don't you think?'

'Zactly,' said the audience solemnly.

Ruth kissed the back of the audience's neck. 'And now!' she cried. Oh, they were clowning for the audience, and if the audience was having fun, so were they!

'Ah *ha!*' Peter made fending, clear-the-decks motions with both hands. He took up his ridiculous garment. Ruth skipped to hold it for him. Peter wiggled in and patted the flying front sections.

'You said it was *tails!*' said the audience in high sweet scorn.

'You don't think so?' said Peter. He put both hands under the coat at the back and suddenly he was marching up and down with a Groucho Marx kind of crouch in his knees and his tails were flapping.

The audience was convulsed. It rolled over in a helpless giggling heap. Bunny wasn't (zactly), thought Ruth, a pretty little girl, but how beautiful she was, laughing! How irresistible!

And she herself gasped, 'Peter, oh stop!'

'O. Jones.'

'Oh, stop! I'll ruin my mascara. Oh *my!*'

The whole long, sweet, slow, mock-solemn ceremony of dressing for The Night crescendoed in hilarity.

Somebody knocked gently on the door.

Something squeezed Ruth's heart, quickly, and as quickly let it go, so that it staggered.

CHAPTER 2

'Mr Jones, here we are, sir,' Eddie's bright blinking eye, the thrust of his neck, were as of a mouse at the door.

'Oh, yes, Eddie. Right on time. How de do. Come in.'

'This here's my niece, Nell Munro. Nell?' Eddie came in, too.

'How de do, Nell.' Peter's tails were a graceful appendage to the Speaker of the Evening. Ruth, herself, moved toward them, the gracious young matron. All the fizz had gone out of the room.

'Good evening, Nell,' she said. 'It was nice of you to come on such short notice. Had you very far?'

'Don't take long on the subway,' Eddie said. His adam's apple jumped. He stood with his skinny shoulders thrust well back. 'Really don't take long at all. She came right straight down.' He seemed proud of this.

The girl, Nell, said nothing. She looked to be nineteen or twenty. She stood demurely with her ankles tight together. Her shoes were shabby black pumps with medium heels. Her head was bent, her lashes lowered. Her hair was the colour of a lion's hide, cut short, not very curly. She wore no hat, a navy blue coat of a conservative cut and a little too big for her. Her hands were folded on a black handbag and Ruth was pleased to see that the nails were bare. Then she hooted at herself for so quaint a connecting of character with nail polish, for after all her own nails were a glossy rose, the shade of her frock. Still . . .

'Won't you take your coat off, Nell?'

11

Eddie said, 'Take your coat off, Nell. Go ahead.'

The girl wore a neat dark silk dress. She held the coat on her arm as if she didn't know what to do with it.

'Just put it here, won't you?' purred Ruth. 'And your bag, too? I suppose you've sat with children before, Nell?'

'She did, back in Indiana,' said Eddie. 'Did it a lot. Not around here so much. She only came east about six months ago.'

'Is that so?'

'She's living with me and my wife, now. My brother's girl . . .'

'And do you like it here, Nell?'

'She likes it fine,' said Eddie. 'We've got room in the apartment, plenty of room for her. My wife's real glad to have her.'

Is the girl mute? Ruth wondered. Eddie's interposing chatter was nervous, as if it covered something lumpish and obstinate in the girl, who was not helping. As one ought to chatter, and push time past this kind of stoppage in its current.

Eddie said, 'What I wannida say, I'll *be* here in the hotel. I mean, I'm going to be around, see? So if you folks are going to be late, you don't need to worry.'

'We may not be so very late,' said Peter smoothly. The effect was as if he said, What are you talking about? He had a towel in one hand and was swiping it recklessly across the shining toes of his evening shoes.

'What I mean,' Eddie blinked, 'I can take Nell home, see?'

Peter looked up, drawled, 'That's nice of you.' Ruth heard his surprised pleasure. The job of taking the sitter home is one of the meanest chores that falls to the lot of the married male. 'But I'd have seen her home, of course,' said Peter virtuously.

Ruth was, at the moment, turning. She thought the pupils moved under the lowered lashes in that bent face. She said, pushing brightly at the sluggishness of things, 'Bunny, dear. Nell, this is Bunny and Bunny, this is Nell.'

'Hello,' said Bunny.

'Hello,' the girl said. Her voice was low and colourless, but at least it worked. She spoke.

'My wife, see,' Eddie was saying, 'took a notion to go to the show so I might's well wait around.' Swallowing made a commotion in his skinny neck. 'We was thinking it might be a real nice idea for Nell. There's a lot of guests bring their children. And me being right here, why, it ought to work out good.'

He showed no sign of going back to his elevator. An anxious little man, the kind who keeps explaining himself, although nobody cares. Terribly concerned to do the right thing. The conscientious kind.

'Suppose we show Nell your room, Bun?' Ruth led them. 'You see, this door can be left a little bit ajar because Bunny does like to go to sleep in the dark. I thought *you* could sit in here, Nell, in our room, where you can be more comfortable.'

Bunny had marched ahead of them into 809. Now she threw one leg possessively over the edge of one of the beds, the one on which her stuffed dog from home was already established.

'Perhaps she ought to turn in quite soon now,' Ruth said gently. 'She's had a pretty exciting day, and to-morrow we have all sorts of plans. Perhaps you'd read her a story? If you don't mind?'

'No, ma'am,' said Nell passively.

'That'll be nice, won't it, Bun?' It *was* like pushing, pushing something heavy. Ruth said with a bright smile, 'Suppose you see if Nell would like some candy.'

Bunny got the box, offered it, as Ruth had taught her, with a gracious little bend of her small body. Nell said, 'Thanks a lot.' And snatched. Ruth felt her heart lighten. Surely that was nice of her. That held some understanding. No grown person could care that much for candy. That greedy quickness must have been exaggerated for the child's sake.

'You're welcome.' Bunny dipped in herself, companionably.

Ruth felt easier. 'Bunny's such a big girl,' she went on, 'there really won't be anything to *do*.' She realized that Eddie's voice and Peter's monosyllables were still going on

13

behind her. 'Bunny's bathroom is over there, of course.' Ruth stepped to dim down the lights, leaving the lamp between the beds. 'And this door,' she waved at the exit from 809 to the correidor, corridor, 'is locked, of course. Now, Bunny's to have one more piece of candy and then she's to brush her teeth and have her story and by that time I expect she'll be pretty sleepy.' She touched the little girl's munching cheek. She looked back through the connecting door.

Eddie's high voice said clearly, 'Well – uh – probably I'll look in on Nell, once in a while, if that's all right with you folks.'

'Surely.' Peter picked up his wallet. Ruth could tell from his back that he was both annoyed and resigned. 'Well – uh – thanks very much.'

'No, sir.' Eddie backed away from the dollar bill. 'No, I'm glad to do it, sir. It's such a good idea for Nell. You just pay her what she earns. Fifty cents an hour. And that'll be fine. That's the arrangement. Nell's mighty glad to have a chance to earn a little something. It's going to work out real nice for her. So – uh – ' he looked rather defiantly past Peter. 'You folks go on out and have a good evening, now.'

Ruth guessed he was speaking to her. 'Thanks very much, Mr Munro. Good night.'

'Good night. Uh – good night. Have a good time now, Mr and Mrs Jones.' His hand hovered in a kind of admonishing gesture. It fell. At last he was gone.

'O.K., Ruth?' said Peter with a touch of impatience.

'In a minute. Nell?' Summoned, the girl moved. Ruth could hear Bunny making a great splutter, brushing her teeth. 'Peter, do you mind looking up the number, where we are going to be? Where we can be reached? We'll just leave it by the phone in here, Nell, and if there is anything at all, why, you *can* call us. You must remember to ask for Peter O. Jones. Don't forget the O. It takes so long to comb out the Joneses otherwise.' She laughed.

Nell said without humour, 'Yes, ma'am.'

Ruth began to turn off lights in 807, leaving only the standing lamp over the big maroon chair and the little lamp between the beds. 'That's enough, Nell?' The girl nodded.

'And if you'd like something to read, there are all these magazines. And please help yourself to the candy. And if you get drowsy, you must lie down in here. I'm sure that will be all right. And,' she lowered her voice discreetly, 'perhaps you had better use this bathroom. Now, is there anything I've forgotten?'

She stood in all her finery, her brow creased just a little, feeling unsatisfied. The girl had said so little. Yet, what was there for her to say? Something, thought Ruth impatiently, some little thing volunteered . . . *anything* to show she's taking hold! 'Can *you* think of anything else?' she prodded.

The girl's head was not so bent any more. Her face was wide at the eyes with high cheek-bones, and the eyes were large and a trifle aslant. Her chin was small and pointed and her mouth was tiny. The face was not made up, and the skin had a creamy yellow-or-peach undertone.

She wasn't bad-looking, Ruth thought with surprise. In fact, she might have been stunning, in an odd provocative way. Even her figure was good under that ill-fitting dress, now that she was standing more erect, not so meekly bent. The eyes were blue. There was too much blue in them, as if the seeing centre were too small, the band of colour wider than it needed to be. The tawny hair straggled over her ears, but Ruth noticed that they were tiny and tight to the head.

'I guess you've thought of everything,' Nell said. The tiny mouth seemed to let itself go into a reluctant, a grudging smile. Her teeth were fine.

Ruth watched her. For just a flash, she wondered if, in that perfectly flat sentence, there had been some mischief lying low, a trace of teasing, a breath of sarcasm.

'Better get going,' Peter moved, full of energy. 'There's the number, Nell, on this paper. Ask them to page us. Doubt if you'll need it. *We* may call up, so if the phone rings . . .' He tapped the slip of paper on the phone table. He started briskly for the closet. The whole world, for Ruth, seemed to take up where it had left off.

Bunny was curled around the jamb of the connecting door, toothpaste lingering on her lips. 'Pop into bed, baby,' Ruth said. 'And Nell will read to you a while.'

Herself in shadow, she watched them obey . . . Bunny peel out of her robe, climb in and pull the covers up, toss her pigtails behind . . . watched the girl move nearer and seat herself tentatively, rather uncertainly, on the edge of the bed, where the light haloed her hair.

Suddenly, Bunny took charge. 'Read me about Jenny and the Twins.' She pitched her book at the girl.

'O.K.,' said Nell, meekly.

Ruth turned away. She bustled, putting things into her evening bag, her wrist watch, her compact, handkerchief, hairpins, lipstick. Her heart was beating a little fast.

Peter was standing silently, with his overcoat on, with her velvet wrap over his arm. She went over and he held it. She looked up at him, wordlessly asked, Is it all right? Wordlessly, he answered, Sure. What can happen? The wrap was soft and cool on her bare arms.

'Eddie's got his eye on,' said Peter in her ear. And she saw, at once, that this was true. Eddie was responsible. Eddie had worked here fourteen years. He couldn't risk losing that record. No. And Eddie was conscientious to a fault. He'd be fussy and watchful. It was Eddie they were hiring, really. He'd have his anxious eye on.

'Take us a while to get across town,' said Peter aloud. Together, they went into the other room. The girl was reading. Her voice was low and monotonous. One word followed another without phrasing. She read like a child.

'All cosy?' said Ruth lightly. 'Night, Bunny.' Her light kiss skidded on the warm little brow.

Peter said, 'Don't forget about your breakfast. So long, honey bun.'

'So long, Daddy. Make a good speech.'

Oh, bless her heart! thought her mother. Oh bless her!

'I'll see what I can do about that, sweetheart,' said Peter tenderly, as touched as she.

The girl sat on the edge of the bed with her finger on her place in the storybook. She watched them go. As they crossed room 807, Ruth heard her voice begin again, ploddingly.

Not all of Ruth went through the door to the corridor. Part remained and tasted the flat, the dim, the silent place

16

from which she had gone. After all the lights and the love and the laughter, how was it for Bunny? Hadn't all the fun too abruptly departed? A part of Ruth lay, in advance of time, in the strange dark. Heard the strange city snarling below. Knew only a stranger's hired meekness was near when something in the night should cry. . . .

Peter put his finger on her velvet shoulder. An elevator was coming. (Not Eddie's, and Ruth was glad. Not again did she wish to hear, 'Have a good time, you folks. Have a good time.')

She shook at her thoughts. She knew what Peter wanted. By her will, she pulled herself together. (Bunny was nine. Bunny would sleep.) She drew the tardy part of herself in toward her body until she was all there, standing by the elevators, dressed to the eyes. She looked up at Peter and showed him she was whole.

It was The Night. At last, it was!

CHAPTER 3

Jed Towers picked up his date at her family's apartment on East Thirty-sixth Street. Her name was Lyn Lesley and she was more than just a date. She had achieved a certain ascendancy on Jed's list. In fact, she was right up there on top. Lyn was slim, dark, with a cute nose and a way of looking out of the corners of her eyes that was neither sly nor flirtatious but simply merry.

He'd known her a year or more, but not until these two weeks, all free time, between jobs, had he seen her so constantly. This had happened easily. A kind of rollicking slide to it. Very smooth and easy to slide from 'see you to-morrow, question mark' to 'see you to-morrow, period' to 'what shall we do to-morrow?' They had fun. Why not? But this next to-morrow Jed was off for the West, all the way to the coast, in fact, where he'd be pinned down a while, in the new job. To-night, their last night, had accumulated without any deliberation on Jed's part the feel of being decisive.

Maybe it wasn't their last night together — but their last night apart. He didn't know. He wasn't stalling. He just didn't know.

They were not in evening clothes. Lyn wore a fuzzy blue coat with big pockets and big buttons and a little blue cap on the back of her head. They decided to walk. They didn't know where they were going, anyway. The mood was tentative and merry . . . no tinge of farewell in it, yet. Lyn hopped and skipped until Jed shortened his stride. They drifted

18

toward the deepest glow in the sky. They might go to a show, might not. It depended.

On Thirty-ninth Street, the block west of Fifth, a beggar accosted them, whining to the girl, 'Help an old man, missus?'

'Oh . . . Jed?' She stood still, impelled to compassion, her face turned up confidently.

Jed's fingers bit her arm. 'Sorry . . .' He dragged her along, 'Just a racket,' he said in her ear. The man's muttering faded in their wake, audible in the shadowy quiet, for the city's noise was, like a fog, thicker afar, never very thick near around you.

She was really dragging her feet. 'How do you know?' she said.

'Know what?' He was surprised. 'Oh, for Lord's sake, Lyn, grow up! That old beetle probably's got more in the bank than we'll ever see.'

'You can't know that,' she said stubbornly.

He stopped walking, astonished. Vaguely, he realized that his brusque decision, back there, might have broken something in her mood, some enchantment maybe. He had no patience with it. He said, 'Now, look. Of course I can't know it, but the chances are, I'm right. You know that. And I don't like being taken for a sucker, Lyn. Now, skip it, shall we?'

She walked along only somewhat more willingly. He said teasingly, 'But you'd have fallen for it, eh? Softie!'

'On the chance he really needed help,' she said in a low voice, 'I'd have risked a quarter.'

'Don't be like that.' Jed laughed at her. 'Sentimental Sue!' He wheeled her into a restaurant. 'This all right?' Jed had been there before. The food was good. He wasn't guessing. He was sorry the mood had been broken. It was his instinct to change the setting, and use the difference and food and drink to bring back whatever it was between them.

They took their table and Jed ordered dinner. Lyn had her lower lip in her teeth, kept her eyes down. When their cock-tails came and he lifted his glass to her, she smiled. She said, 'I'm not sentimental, Jed. It isn't that.'

'No?' He wished she'd skip it. He, himself, was finished with that trivial moment. 'Drink your drink, honey.' He smiled at her. When the cool beauty of his face broke, in his smile, to affectionate attention, it pulled on the heart of the beholder. Jed did not know that, in such terms. But he knew, of course, statistically, that what he offered was not often rejected.

But Lyn said, wanly, 'You have an awfully quick way of mistrusting people.' Her voice was gentle but he thought there were stormy signs in her eyes and anger stirred in Jed's own.

He said, evenly, gently, 'I didn't think you were that childish, Lyn. I really didn't.'

'I can't see,' she said, holding scorn out of the voice carefully, 'how it would have hurt. Two bits. Or even a dime.'

'Spare a dime,' he mocked. 'For Lord's sake, Lyn, let's not fight about it.'

'No.' She pushed her glass to and fro on the cloth and she smiled. 'But you do expect the worst of people, don't you, Jed? I've . . . noticed.'

'Certainly,' he grinned. 'You damn well better, as far as I can see.' He offered her his certainty with careless cheer.

She took a deep swallow of her drink, set down the glass, and looked across the room. 'I don't think I care for cheap cynicism,' she said.

'Cheap!' he exploded. Women were the limit! What a thing to come out with, just like that! He realized he must have hurt her, somehow. But he also knew he hadn't meant to. 'For Lord's sake!' he said, 'that's about the most expensive piece of education I ever got myself. I'd hate to tell you what I had to pay for it.' He was still genuinely astonished.

'You don't believe . . .' she began and her lips were trembling.

'Don't believe!' he scoffed. 'Listen – aw, you baby! What I believe or what you believe makes no particular difference to the way things are. Lyn, honey, sooner or later you get to know that. All the difference it makes is whether you're comfortable or not. Well, it just happens I don't like to be fooled and I've got to the point where I don't even enjoy fooling myself.' She flicked her lashes. 'This,' he said soberly, 'is a pretty stinking lousy world.'

'Is it?' said Lyn.

He was annoyed. 'If you haven't noticed that, you're unintelligent,' he said crisply.

'And what do you do about it?'

'Mind your own business. Take care of yourself, because you can be damn sure nobody else will. Lyn, for the love of Mike, let it go, will you? Anybody thinks *he* can save the world isn't weaned yet. You're old enough to know that much.'

'If everybody figured the way you do . . .' she began, looking unhappy.

'You like the boy-scout type?' he challenged. 'The sunshine kids?'

'No.'

'The dreamy boys? The old stars in the eyes?'

'Stop it!'

'O.K.,' he said. 'So I'm not going to water myself down and play pat-a-cake with you.' He cancelled his anger. He offered, again, his smile and himself.

'I don't want you to,' she said. 'I'm interested in what you think about things.' Her voice was low again.

'But you don't think much of my way of thinking?' he said, more challenging than he had intended to be. 'Is that it?'

She turned her hand.

'Well . . .' he shrugged. 'I'm sorry, honey, but one thing that stinks high in this lousy world is the lip service to sweetness and light. Everybody's for it. But does their left hand know what their lip is saying?' At least, I'm honest, his eyes were saying. I'm telling you. 'Look, I didn't expect an inquiry into my philosophy of life. I thought this was a date . . . you know, for fun?'

Her lips parted. He read in her look that they both knew it wasn't just a date . . . for fun. But she didn't speak.

'Show?' he said lightly. If they went to a show, it would deny, somehow, their ability to be together. He felt that, suddenly.

She said, 'In such a stinking lousy world, what do you expect?'

'Oh, say, the love of a good woman,' he answered lightly, because he *didn't* want to discuss this kind of thing seriously any more. And then he was sorry. He saw her lips whiten. He'd hurt her, again, when all he wanted was to get lightly off the subject. 'Aw, Lyn, please . . . What are we yapping about? How'd we get off?'

'Coffee now?' inquired the waiter.

'Coffee, honey?' Jed put his hand on hers.

'Please,' she said, not smiling. But it seemed to him that her hand was on his and he thought if he could kiss her, hard, right now, it would be a fine thing.

Bunny listened politely to the story. When Mommy read, the story seemed more interesting. When Daddy read to her it was interesting too, although Daddy never did finish a story. He always got off to explaining something, and the explaining turned out to be *another* story. She sat quietly against her pillow, her stuffed dog under her arm, until the voice stopped. Nell looked at her, then. 'I better go to sleep, now,' said Bunny, 'I guess.'

'O.K.' The mattress moved, the spring changed shape, as Nell stood up.

'I can turn off my light,' said Bunny kindly.

'O.K. then,' Nell said. She put the book down on the other bed. She walked away. She picked up the candy box, looked once over her shoulder, and went through the door.

Bunny snapped off the light, watched the pattern of shadows establish itself. She wondered if the window was open. Nell hadn't looked to see. The room felt stuffy and dusty hot. Bunny wasn't quite sure she knew how to work the Venetian blind. She lay still quite a long time, but it didn't feel right to go to sleep, not knowing whether the window was open. She sneaked her feet out and felt the bristles of the carpet. She fumbled with the thin ropes and after a while there was a soft rattle and the slats changed. Now, she could see. The window *was* open. It was all right then. Bunny crept back under the blankets. The air smelled dusty, just the same, and the pillow didn't smell like her pillow at home either. Bunny pushed her nose into it and lay still.

Nell set the communicating door at an angle that almost

closed it. Then she stood absolutely still, tipping her head as if to listen. Room 809 was quiet, behind her. Room 807 was a pool of silence. Her eyes shifted. The big lamp flooded the spot near the windows where the big chair stood. The small lamp touched the upper ends of the twin beds. Elsewhere there were shadows.

Nell put the candy box down on a bed and walked back with a silent gliding step to the windows and tripped the blind. The court was too narrow to see very far up or down. Across, there was only one lighted window. The blind there was up a third of the way, and she could see the middle section of a woman, seated at the desk. A black and white belt marked a thick waist on a black dress. There was nothing else to see. Not many spent their evenings in, at the Hotel Majestic.

Nell pivoted, glided in that same step to the middle of room 807 and stood still. She did not stand still long. Although her feet remained in the same flower of the carpet pattern, they began to dance. The heels lifted and fell fractions of an inch, only, as her weight shifted. Her hips rolled softly, and her shoulders and her forearms. Her fingers were the most active part of her body in this dance. They made noiseless snaps and quick restless writhings of their own. Her chin was high and her head, swaying with the tiny movements of her body, wove the pattern of a wreath in the silent air.

Meantime Nell's eyes, wide open, darted as she danced. Very alive and alert they were. Her whole face was vivid, more sly than shy, not in the least demure.

In a little while, the feet danced daintily, in the tiniest of steps, off the one flower. Nell swooped over Peter's suitcase. Her hand, impiously, not tentatively at all, scooped through its contents. Handkerchiefs and ties flew like sand from a beach castle. There were some letters and a manila folder flat on the bottom. The girl snatched them out, opened the folder awkwardly, and all the paper slid out in a limp curve. She stood with the empty folder in her hands and looked down at the spilled papers in the suitcase. Then she yanked the letters from the clip that held them to the folder. They didn't interest her for long. She dropped all the papers out of her hands, as if it were merely paper, with no other meaning. She flipped the lid of the suitcase with one finger and it fell.

She made three long steps and pivoted with one leg out like a dancer's, pulling it slowly around. She sat down, with an effect of landing there by sheer accident, on the bench in front of the dressing-table. Ruth had turned the two little lamps out. It did not seem to occur to Nell to switch them on. She rummaged in Ruth's box of jewellery. There were three bracelets and Nell clasped them all on her left arm. There were two brooches and she pinned one above the other on the left lapel of her dress. There were a string of coral-coloured beads, and Ruth's three-strand pearls, and a silver locket on a silver chain. All these Nell took up and fastened around her neck. A pair of tiny turquoise and silver earrings that matched one of the pins she put at her ears. She looked at herself in the shadowy glass, solemnly, lumpishly. She smiled. Slowly, she began to take everything off again. As she removed each piece she did not return it to its place in the box. When the table-top was scattered with most of the things, Nell seemed to lose interest. She still wore the earrings.

She turned, very slowly, sliding around, moving her legs as if they were in one piece. She kicked off her black pumps. Ruth's aquamarine mules with the maribou cuffs were standing neatly under the dressing-table. Nell put her feet into them. She rose and walked up and down in them, watching her feeting, acquiring more and more skill and arrogance in the ankles and the arches. At last, she seemed almost strutting. Then she seemed to forget, and moved about as easily as if the mules had long been her own.

She ate three pieces of candy, slowly.

Then she sat down on the bench again and picked up Ruth's perfume. The tiny glass stick, attached to the stopper, she discarded. She tipped the bottle on her forefinger and dabbed the forefinger behind her ears. She held the forefinger under her nostrils and inhaled dreamily, swaying to and fro as if she tantalized her own senses in a dreamy rhythm. The little bottle dropped out of her left hand, cracked on the table top, lay on its side. The liquid began to seep out among the jewellery. (The twelve dollars that had been Peter's, the fifty cents that had been Bunny's, last Mother's Day.)

Nell noticed it, finally. Her face did not change. She picked up Ruth's hairbrush, dipped it, making a smearing motion, in the spilled perfume, and began to brush her tawny hair. She brushed it sharply back from her ears. Now her face took on another look. Now the shape of it, the sharp taper to the chin, the subtle slant of the eye sockets, became older, more sleek, reptilian.

She drew the hairbrush once around her throat.

She rose and walked between the beds, turned, and let herself fall supine on the one to the left of the telephone. After a little while she lifted her right arm, languidly, letting her hand dangle from the wrist, looking up at her fingers that hung limp off the palm.

Then she sat up, propped her back with pillows, and opened the fat phone book. She opened it almost at the centre and looked at the pages with unfocused eyes. She lifted her left hand and dropped it on the fine print. Where her left forefinger-nail fell she gouged a nick in the paper.

She picked up the phone with her right hand, asked sweetly for the number.

'Yes?' A man's voice came out of the city, somewhere, hooked and caught at the end of the wire.

'Guess who?' Nell said in a soft high soprano.

'Margaret, where are – '

'Oh-ho no! Not Margaret!'

'Who is this?' said the voice irritably. 'I'm not in the mood – '

'By the way, who *is* Margaret? Hmmmmmmmm?'

'Margaret is my wife,' said the voice stiffly. 'What's the idea?'

'Ha!'

'Who is this?'

'Virginia,' crooned Nell. 'Don't you remember me?'

'I think you have the wrong number,' the voice said, sounding very old and tired, and he hung up.

Nell sucked her cheeks in, turned pages, gave another number.

'Hello?' A woman this time.

'Hello. Oh, hello. Is Mr Bennet there?'

'No, he's not. I'm sorry.' Brightly. 'This is *Mrs* Bennet.'

'Oh,' said Nell without alarm. With nothing. Flatly. Her head tilted listening.

'Can I take a message?' the woman said, somewhat less cordially.

'Oh, dear,' simpered Nell. 'You see, this is Mr Bennet's secretary . . .'

'Mr Bennet has no secretary that I know of.'

'Oh,' said Nell. 'Oh dear me! Are you sure?'

'Who is this?' The voice began to sound as if the face were red.

'Just a friend. You know?'

'Will you give me your name, please?'

'Why, no,' said Nell flatly and then she giggled.

The phone slammed shut at the other end. On Nell's face danced a look of delighted malice.

She stretched. She called the girl downstairs again. 'Long distance.'

'One moment, please.'

Rochelle Parker, at the switchboard, was efficient and indifferent. She dealt with the barrage of calls from 807 for a long time without much comment, even to herself. She got in on part of a wrangle between the long-distance operator and whoever was calling, up there, over the existence of an exchange in Chicago. The person upstairs used language, softly. It was as bad as Rochelle had ever heard over the wires and she'd heard some. And this was worse, sounding so hushed-like.

'Jeepers,' said Rochelle to herself. The eyebrows that Rochelle, herself, had remodelled from nature's first idea went up to her bangs. It crossed her mind that she might say a word to Pat Perrin, the house detective. Probably, she thought, they were drinking, up there. People had a few, and went on telephone jags, sometimes.

She decided it was none of her business. What went over the wire wasn't disturbing the sacred peace of the Hotel

26

Majestic. If 807 began to do that, somebody else would catch on.

And the telephone bill would be part of the hangover. 'Oh, boy,' she thought and grinned. Then 807 suddenly quit calling.

The phone book had fallen off the bed. Nell rolled over on her stomach and looked at it, lying on the carpet.

She sat up, curling her legs under her. She yawned. She listened. Her rambling glance passed the half-open closet door and returned . . .

CHAPTER 4

A tall man looks best in tails, they say. Ruth thought that, although Peter O. Jones was not too terribly tall, he looked wonderful. She saw no man there who looked more distinguished than he. Erect, compact, controlled, he walked beside her. And if the bold lines of his face were not handsome, they were better than that. People remembered Peter.

She saw herself, too, in the mirror walls of the passage to the ballroom and she began to walk as if she were beautiful. For the frock was becoming and in the soft light she even liked her nose. Maybe it did turn up, as Peter insisted, against all evidence, that it did. At least it had, as he said, the air of being *about* to turn up, any minute.

Her hand with the rosy nails pressed the black cloth of his left sleeve and Peter crossed his right arm over and touched her hand. Here they stood, at the portal. Black and white men, multi-coloured ladies, flowers, table-and-chairs like polka dots over the floor, but the long white bar of the speakers' table dominated.

'Peter O. Jones,' said her husband very quietly to somebody. A black back bent. They followed toward the speakers' table and Ruth could see their path, opening, and the turning faces marked it as if flowers were being thrown under their feet.

Somebody stepped into their way, holding out his hand. 'Peter O. Jones?' he said joyfully. 'Want you to meet . . .' 'Beg pardon, sir, but this is . . .' 'How do you do?' *Mrs* Jones, ah . . .' They were in a cluster. Yet they were moving slowly, surely, toward the speakers' table. Peter had the nicest *way* about him. So many people knew who he *was*. Ruth struggled to remain balanced, to lock names to faces. It was confusing! It was glorious!

Jed and Lyn were still sitting in the restaurant. Coffee, brandy, more coffee, and many cigarettes had gone by. They'd had no ambition to stir themselves, to go to a show. They were caught in the need to settle something. Maybe it was never to be settled. This was what they needed to know. Jed shared, now, Lyn's feeling that it was important. They were hanging on to their tempers, both of them.

They'd about finished, speaking awkwardly, obliquely for the most part, with God.

'What I know,' he said, 'the Lord ain't Santa Claus. You got them mixed, honey. Santa Claus, sure, *he'll* open his pack if you been a good girl. I don't think it's the same.' His brows made angles.

'You don't believe in it at all,' she said wearily.

'I don't nag myself about it.' He shrugged.

'All I'm trying to say, Jed,' she was making an effort to be sweet, 'is just this. I'd like . . . all right, call it soft . . . call it anything you want . . . I'd have *liked* it, if you had given that old man a coin. What would it matter if he really needed it or not? It would have been good for *us*.'

'Aw, that's junk, Lyn. Pure junk.'

'It isn't junk!'

His voice slipped. Damned-up irritation slipped out. 'It's ridiculous!'

Her eyes flashed. They had worked to smile, too long. 'I'm glad to know you think I'm ridiculous.'

'Maybe it's a good idea to know these things,' he agreed coldly. 'You called me a cheap cynic, remember?'

'And perhaps you are,' she said shortly, 'just that.'

'It's no chore of mine, Lyn,' he fought to sound reasonable, 'to contribute to the income of a perfect stranger who's done nothing for me.'

'It's not a question of your responsibility. It's your charity.'

'Nuts to that kind of charity. I intend to earn what I get . . .'

'People can't always. There's such a thing as being helpless . . . through no fault . . .'

'The rule is, you get what you pay for, pay for what you get. You grow up, you know that.'

'Suppose *you* needed food . . . or a place to . . .'

'Then,I go beg from organized charities who recognize that so-called helplessness and, incidentally, check up on it to see if it is real. *I'll* never expect a stranger on the street to shell out for me. Why should he? Why should he believe me? It works both ways. You look out for yourself in this world, that's all I . . .'

'It's not true! People have to believe . . .'

'Why?'

'Why anything, then?' she blazed. 'What are you living for?'

'How do I know? I didn't put me here. Of all the idiotic —'

'I think you'd better take me home.'

Their voices came to a dead stop.

'Why?' he said finally, his eyes glittering.

'Because this isn't fun.'

'Why should I take you home?' he said, smouldering. 'Ask some kind stranger.'

She stared. She said, 'You're quite right. I do nothing for you. Or your ego. Do I? I'll be leaving now.'

'Lyn . . .'

'Yes?' she said icily, half up, her coat on her shoulders.

'If you go . . .'

'Why should I not? You're not entertaining me. Nothing's for free, you say.'

'If you go . . .'

'I know. We'll never meet again. Is that it?'

'That's it, I'm afraid.'

'Jed, I don't want to . . .' She was more limp, more yielding.

'Then for Lord's sake,' he said irritably, assuming it was all over, 'sit down and quit talking like a little jackass.'

Her sideways glance was not merry at all. 'Good night,' she said quietly.

He settled in the chair, took a cigarette out of the package.

'Got your mad money? Here.' He threw a five-dollar bill on the tablecloth.

Lyn's lips drew back from her teeth. He could feel, like a strong sudden gust, her impulse to hit him. Then he thought she'd cry.

But she walked away.

He sat, staring at the messy table. Of all the stinking lousy dates he ever had in his life! Protectively, he thought of it as just a date. He was furious. He advanced to being outraged. His last night in this town! Last night in the East! Last date! And she walked out on him.

For what? He oversimplified. Because he didn't give that mangy old deadbeat a quarter. Of all the . . . ! He sat there and let anger become a solid lump. After a while he paid the check and put his coat on. Outside, he looked east, then west. Lyn was nowhere about.

He began to walk, fast, hands dug in his coat pockets. He supposed gloomily it was a good thing he'd found out what kind of stuff passed for thought in her head. (Lyn, with the dark head, his shoulder high.) So . . . cross *her* off the list. Yeah. Couldn't she see he hadn't tried to hurt her? Couldn't she concede he'd learned a few things, formed some opinions, had to have a core of conviction that was, at least, honestly come by? No, she couldn't. So she walked away.

But Towers would have a date to-night, just the same. His little book (with the list) was at the hotel, damn it. He swung north. Hadn't thought he'd need it. But he *had* it. He could put his hand on it. His pride, his proof, his very honour began to get involved here. Towers would have a date his last night. Wouldn't be stood up, not he!

Jed slammed through the revolving door. It stuttered, not moving as fast as he. He stood, towering, teetering, smouldering, at the desk, crisply after his key. He went up to the eighth floor, unlocked his door, put on his light, flung off his coat, in one swift surge of entering.

He visited the bathroom.

He came out with the bathroom glass in his hand and stared around him. He dipped into his bag for that bottle of rye. He could think of nobody on his list who'd do him good.

And the preliminaries. He was in no mood for them. Call any girl, this time of night, and you could hear her little brain buzzing. Oh, will I look unpopular if I admit I'm not busy? They all wondered, the nit-wits. So she'd say she had a date. And he'd say, 'Break it for me?' Knowing damn well she probably was just about to wash her hair or something. so, she'd 'break it'. Phoney. Everything was pretty phoney.

(Not Lyn. She was just too naïve to live.)

He looked at the telephone. Call her and apologize? But what was there, honestly, to apologize for? He'd only said things he believed. He couldn't change his spots. They'd only start over again. They didn't think the same. And nobody walked out on Towers twice! This, she'd find out.

Aw, quit stewing.

The blind across his bank of windows was not drawn. He realized that he stood as one on a lighted stage. It felt, too, as if eyes were upon him. Somebody was watching him.

He moved toward the windows that looked out on a court.

He was looking directly across the narrow dark deep well into another lighted bank of windows. The other room hung there in the night like a lighted stage. The scene had no depth. It was lit by a lamp near the windows. The light fell on a female figure. There was a girl or a woman over there. She was dressed in some kind of flowing bluish or greenish thing. She seemed to be sitting *in* the window, probably on the flat top of the long radiator cover. Her neck was arched. She had short yellowish hair. She seemed to be looking down at a point on her right leg just above the knee. A garter or something? Her right foot rested on the radiator top. The nicely-shaped leg was bent there, framed and exhibited, with the bluish-green fabric flowing away from it.

She was not looking out, not looking at him. He was absolutely certain that she had been. He knew he must be silhouetted in the frame of his own windows. He stood still, watching her, making no further move to pull his blind down. He was absolutely certain that she knew he was there.

She moved her right palm slowly down the curve of her calf. Her head turned. She looked across at him. He did not move.

Neither did she.

Her hand rested on her ankle. Her garment remained as it was, flowing away from the pretty knee. Her head was flung up from the neck. She looked at him.

There was something so perfectly blunt about the two of them, posed as they were, each in his bright box, suspended, aware . . . It was as if a shouted *Well?* crossed the court between them.

Jed felt himself grin. The anger that hummed in his veins changed pitch, went a fraction higher. What was this? and why not? he thought, pricked and interested.

CHAPTER 5

The girl took her hand from her ankle, put both hands on the radiator top behind her, bent her body to lean back on the stiff support of both her arms, kept looking out at him. There was something direct about it that fitted with his mood.

Jed was reading the floor plan of the hotel that lay in his head. He was counting off numbers, calculating. He had the kind of mind that carried maps and floor plans with him always. He felt pretty sure he knew what the number of that room must be. He put his bottle of rye down and raised both hands where the shape of them would be silhouetted for her to see. He signalled with eight fingers, with both hands bent in an O, and then with seven fingers.

She sat up, suddenly, wrapped both arms around her middle, and turned so that the knee slid down. She was facing him, her head tilted as if to say, What do you mean?

He took up the bottle in his left hand, pointed at it, at her, at himself.

Her chin went high, as if her head fell back in laughter.

He put down the bottle, pantomimed himself at a telephone. She understood because her head turned and she looked behind her toward where the phone in that room must be.

She made the sign of seven.

Jed backed away from the window. He knew he was still perfectly visible, perhaps even plainer to her sight now, in the glare of the overhead light. He picked up his phone. He said to the girl, '807 please.'

Downstairs, as Rochelle made the connexion, a thought no clearer than the word 'huh?' crossed her mind fleetingly. Pursuing it, she remembered. Oh yeah, 807 was the whispering foul-mouth. What now? Probably, she surmised, 821 was going to complain. She was tempted. She heard a man's voice say, 'Well?' It was blunt and a trifle mocking. It wasn't going to complain. Rochelle's interest, faint in the first place, faded. The muscles of her mouth made a quick cynical comment, soon forgotten.

Jed could still see the girl, in the little puddle of light by the beds in there, answering her phone. He waved. 'Hi,' he said, over the wire.

She made a soft sound, like a chuckle. 'Hello.'

'*Would* you like a drink?'

'I might,' she said.

'Alone?'

She knew what he was asking. 'You can see, can't you?' she said and the hint of laughter came again.

'If I walk around, will you open the door?'

'I might.'

'It's a long walk,' he said.

He had the impression that she would have teased him, but something happened. He saw her head turn. Some sound . . . that she could hear but he could not. She said, in a different mood and a different tempo, 'Wait a few minutes?'

'This is an impulse,' Jed said frankly. 'It might not last.'

'Five minutes,' she said, sounding eager and conspiratorial now. 'There's somebody at the door.' Then she said, 'Oh, please,' softly and very softly hung up.

Jed sat on the bed in his room, and automatically put the phone down. He saw her at the window, lowering the blind, but she tripped it so that he could still see into the room. He knew when she went into the shadowy part, when she opened the door. The visitor came in the direction that, to Jed, was downstage, came in far enough so that he could identify the hotel livery.

Bellhop, or something. Oh, well . . . He went into his bathroom with a vague sense of stepping into the wings for a moment, out of the footlights. He looked at himself in the glass. His anger was no longer so solid. It had broken into a rhythmic beat. It came and went, ebbed and flowed. When it pulsed high he felt reckless and in a mood to smash. When it ebbed low he felt a little bit blank and tired. But the pulse was strong, the beat was urgent. It seemed necessary to do something.

Eddie said, 'Little girl went to sleep, all right, did she? You all right, Nell?'

'Umhum,' Nell murmured. She'd fallen into the maroon chair and looked relaxed there. Her lids fell as if they were heavy over her eyes. Her face was smooth and seemed sleepy.

'What you got on? Nell!' Eddie's voice was thin and careful.

'I'm not hurting anything.'

Eddie's flitting eye caught the top of the dressing-table and the condition it was in. His gold-flecked teeth bit over his pale lip. He moved closer to the dressing-table. After a while he said in a low voice, 'You shouldn't monkey with other people's stuff, Nell. Really, you shouldn't.'

'I'm not hurting anything,' she repeated and her voice was more truculent than before.

Eddie gnawed his lip. He rescued the perfume bottle and replaced the stopper. Almost furtively, his fingers began to neaten the tumble of jewellery. He began to talk, softly, coaxingly.

'It's kind of an easy job, though, isn't it, Nell? Don't you think so? Just to sit for a few hours in a nice room like this. And just think, you get paid for it. Fifty cents an hour isn't bad, for nothing but being here. If you was home, you'd be sitting around with Aunt Marie, waiting for bedtime, just the same. You like it, don't you, Nell?'

'Oh, sure,' she said drowsily.

'Nell, you . . . better take off that negligee . . . and the slippers. Honest. I don't think Mrs Jones would like that.'

'She won't know the difference,' said Nell shortly.

'Well,' said Eddie, 'I hope you . . . Will you take them off, like a good girl?'

'Umhum,' she murmured. 'Sure I will, Uncle Eddie,' She lifted her eyes and smiled at him.

He was enormously encouraged and pleased. 'That's right,' he cried. 'That's good. Take them off, Nell, and put them where they were, so she won't know. Because you want to get paid. You want to get more jobs like this. Don't you see, Nell? It'll be a real nice kind of little work for you. So easy. And you can do what you want with the money, after. You can buy some fancy slippers like those for *yourself*, Nell. Or a pair of earrings. Wouldn't that be nice?'

She turned her cheek to the chair.

Eddie wished he knew how it was Marie talked to her, what it was she did. Because Nell was good when Marie was around, real quiet and good.

'Tell you what I'll do,' he said heartily. 'When I get off duty, I'll bring you up a coke. O.K.? Have a little refreshment, you and me. It won't seem so long. You'll be surprised how the time will go by.'

'Sleepy,' she murmured.

'Well,' he said, bracing his shoulders, 'nap a little bit. That's a good idea.' He looked at the perfume bottle that was now nearly empty. He cleared his throat. He said in a nervous rush, 'And you ought to apologize for spilling the perfume . . . right away when she comes back.'

Nell's lids went up slowly until her eyes were very wide. 'It was an accident,' she said an octave higher than before. Her whole body had tightened.

'I know, I know,' said Eddie quickly. He stepped near her and put a gentle hand on her shoulder. She twisted away from it. 'Of course it was an accident. I believe you, Nell. Sure it was. The only thing I mean is, it's a good idea to say so, real soon, before she notices. Anybody can have an accident like that. She won't blame you.'

Nell said nothing.

'It'll be all right,' said Eddie, comfortingly. 'You couldn't help it. Now, you just – just take it easy a little bit. I'll be back.' He looked nervously behind him. The open elevator, standing too long on the eighth floor, was present in his consciousness. 'I gotta go. But you're all right, aren't you?'

He swallowed. 'Please, Nell,' he said in a thin pleading voice, 'don't get into no more mischief with their things!'

'I'm not doing anything,' she said sullenly.

But, when he sighed and paused in his progress toward the door as if he would plead some more, she said quickly, 'I'm sorry, Uncle Eddie. I'll put everything back. You know I get . . . restless.' Her hands moved to the earrings. 'I'll take them off.'

Immediately, he was pleased. 'Sure, I know you get restless. I know you don't mean anything. I want you to . . . kinda get used to this idea. The thing is, to *think*, Nell. We could work up a kind of a little business, here. If you'd just . . . if you like it.'

'I do like it,' she said, sounding thoughtful and serious. An earring lay in her hand.

The little man's face reddened with his delight. 'Good girl! That's swell! And it's a date, now. Don't forget. I'll bring the cokes.' And so he withdrew, pointed little face going last, like a mouse drawing back into its hole.

Nell waited for the door to close. With no expression on her face she put the earring back on her ear lobe. She got slowly to her feet. Then they began to move on the carpet in that tiny dance. She listened. She went to the blind and it rattled up under her hands.

Jed was standing in the middle of his room, his weight even on both feet, looking rather belligerently across at her.

She flung up both arms in a beckoning gesture, let them go on, until her arms were in a dancer's high curve, and she whirled backward from the window. Jed stood still. And the girl stood still, posed with her arms high, looking over her shoulder.

In a second, Jed put the bottle in his pocket, and his finger on his light switch. His light went out.

Nell pawed, disturbing the order Eddie had created and she snatched at Ruth's spare coral lipstick.

CHAPTER 6

Jed's impulse had been flickering like a candle in a draught. He put the bottle in his pocket for the necessary little drink that you take while you look the situation over, put his key in his pocket, too, heard the elevator gate closing. So he waited for the faint hum of its departure before he went around the corner to his right and passed the elevators and turned right again.

His mood was cautious when he tapped on the door marked 807.

She was not very tall, not very old, not bad-looking either. But he couldn't type her. No curly blonde. Not a sleek blonde. Her face, tilted to look at him, was a triangle and the eyes were set harlequin-wise. Jed's nostrils moved. She reeked . . . the whole room reeked . . . of perfume. She opened the door wider, quickly. He took a step and the door closed behind him as if she had fanned him into this perfumed place. His glance went rapidly around. He looked, and knew it, as if he were ready to take the step back again, and out.

'What's in the bottle?' she asked.

He took it out of his pocket and showed her the label. He said, mechanically, 'Too nice a night to drink alone.' His cool grey stare examined her.

Her blue eyes examined his. For a minute, he thought there wasn't going to be any act . . . and he was fascinated by that same sense of blunt encounter that he had felt before.

This wasn't a type he knew.

She turned, tripping a little on the aquamarine hem of the

negligee, so long it puddled on the floor around her. She said, 'Won't you sit down?' Her voice was flat and matter-of-fact. Yet he wasn't sure whether she used a cliché or mocked one.

He set the bottle on the desk and walked past it, going warily to the big maroon chair. 'Nice of you to let me come over,' he said, perfunctorily. His eye caught certain signs and he was not pleased. He thought he had better get out of here as gracefully as was quick. Obviously, this room was half a man's.

She walked over a bed on her knees and then was standing between the two of them with complete dignity. It was an odd effect, almost as if she didn't notice how she had got there, as if she assumed that of course she must have walked around the bed like a lady. She put her hands on the phone. 'We must have some ice,' she said grandly.

'Fine.'

'Ginger ale?'

The name on the envelope caught in the hasp of the suitcase was Jones. 'Whatever you like, Mrs Jones,' Jed said.

She was startled. Her body stiffened as she held herself high in surprise. Then her reddish lashes swept down. Into the phone she said, grandly, 'Please send ice and ginger ale to Mrs Jones in 807.'

Jed guessed she was being some movie star or other. But they'd cut a line out of the picture. She forgot to ask for room service. The operator obliged. Looking over Jed's head, posed like a model for a photograph of glamour, the girl repeated her order with exactly the same inflections. It was mimicry, all right.

But when she hung up her whole face changed. 'I'm not Mrs Jones,' she told him with sly delight. 'Mrs Jones went out.' This wasn't mimicry. It was . . . odd.

Jed looked mildly interrogative.

'This isn't my room,' she chuckled.

He thought to himself that this was no worse a dodge than any. 'That's funny. The room over there isn't *my* room, either. Coincidence?' He leaned back, grinning.

'Mr and Mrs Jones went out,' she said frowning.

'The fellow whose room I was in went out, too,' said Jed,

still grinning. 'He's got a date.' He felt anger pulse in his neck and jaw. 'Lucky guy. Or is he? Or am I?'

She sat down on the bed and stuffed a pillow behind her. 'I'm going to South America to-morrow,' she remarked lightly.

'Oh? What part?' She didn't answer. 'I'm off to Europe myself,' he lied cheerfully. He didn't believe a word she'd said so far.

'Mr Jones is my brother,' said the girl. 'I hate him. I hate all my relatives. They won't let me do anything. They don't want me to have dates.' She looked both dreamy and sullen. Jed began to believe some of this. Something was real about it.

'Shall we make it a date?' he suggested. 'Would you like to go dancing?'

Her head jerked. He saw her quick desire to go and her recollection of some reason why not . . . the jump of a flame and its quick quenching. 'I haven't any evening clothes,' she said, and he gawped at such an excuse. If excuse it was. 'Mrs Jones had a beautiful evening dress.'

'Your . . . sister-in-law?'

'And a velvet wrap the colour of this.' She touched the negligee. 'You can't buy that for fifty cents an hour.'

Jed made no sense of what she was saying. A rap on the door cut into his puzzling. Boy with the ice. Jed got up and turned his back, looking out through the blind as if there was something to see. There was nothing to see but some old biddy writing letters over there. Jed hardly noticed even that. He was annoyed by the notion that he ought not let himself be seen in here.

Still, a hotel, he guessed, in its official consciousness, usually knew by some nervous sympathy what went on within its walls. It pounced or it did not pounce. But it knew. Probably he wasn't fooling anybody.

'Sign, miss.' The boy was mumbling.

The girl was at a complete loss. She had never seen this in the movies. Her grand air was punctured. She didn't know anything about signing a check.

Jed turned around. 'Better let me get it, honey.' He fumbled for money. 'What time did your brother go out?' he asked her over his shoulder.

She said nothing.

'Do *you* know?' Jed watched the boy's worldly young eyes. 'Notice a couple in evening clothes? She wore a wrap, that colour.'

'Mr and Mrs Jones?' said the boy smoothly. 'Yeah, they left quite a long while ago.'

'How long will they be?' Jed asked the girl.

She shrugged. 'Some shindig . . .'

'Yeah? Well . . .' Jed watched the boy whose eyes were first satisfied, then veiled. The boy took his tip and departed.

The boy, whose name was Jimmy Reese, went down the corridor jauntily, his lips pursed to whistle, shaping a tune without the breath to make it audible. Eddie's elevator picked him up. They eyed each other with a kind of professional contempt. Jimmy's whistle went right on.

The guy in 807 belonged in 821. This Jimmy knew. Who that girl was, Jimmy did not know. So she was Jones's sister. For all he knew. He didn't know she had anything to do with Eddie. He looked up at the grill-work, coming to the chorus. He didn't think 821 was looking for Jones in there, though. Jimmy kept a lot of amusing things to himself.

Eddie didn't know that Jimmy had just been to 807. He'd listened hard at the eighth floor. He'd eyed the boy. All seemed quiet.

So they sank down, professionally aloof, exchanging no comments, no gossip, no information.

Jed, fixing drinks, thought it over. He hadn't been trying to set up a picture of himself, the dropper-in who had missed his host. He guessed he wasn't fooling anybody. On the other hand, he had established something. Mr and Mrs Jones *had* gone out. Who was this, then?

'You got a name?' he asked gently.

'Nell.' She told him so absent-mindedly he believed it was true.

Nevertheless, he lied, saying, 'I'm John.' He handed her a glass.

She took a deep swallow, looked up, and laughed at him. 'You don't know what to think about me. You're nervous. You're funny.'

He let it ride. He went over and fixed the blind. Then he sat down on the bed next to her. 'Where you from, Nell?'

'California.'

'What part?'

'All of it.'

'You can't do that. California's too big.'

'It's not so big.'

'San Francisco?'

'Sometimes.'

'Tulsa?' he said.

'There, too,' she answered serenely. She was rolling this stuff off the top of her head, not even bothering to make sense.

'Where is Tulsa?' he asked, in sudden suspicion.

'In California.' She looked surprised.

'Nell,' he said amiably, 'you're a liar.'

'Oh, well,' she said, suddenly soft as a kitten, leaning against his arm, 'you're lying to me, too.'

'I haven't said anything.'

'You're lying, just the same.'

He took her chin in his left hand, turned her face and searched it and his pulse jumped, recognizing the cockeyed honesty there. You're a liar. I'm a liar. Well? No, it wasn't a look, given cynically, after long practice. There was something perfectly fresh about it.

She was not a type he knew.

'Well?' he said, aloud. He bent his mouth to kiss her.

The taste of her lips was very close when a ripple went down his spine. He turned Nell's quietly waiting face with his hand, pressing it to his shoulder. His neck worked stiffly, slowly. He looked behind.

There was a little girl with dark pigtails, barefooted, in pink pyjamas. She was watching them silently.

A wild animal could have startled him no more.

43

CHAPTER 7

The shock seemed to lift him into the air. He croaked, controlling his voice better than his reflexes, 'Seems to be an audience.' He had pushed Nell to her balance. He had pivoted without straightening his knees. He was suddenly sitting on the other bed, facing the child . . . reaching for his glass. . . .

Jed, going about his business, brushed by the children in the world without making any contact. They didn't interest him. Like philatelists or monks or surrealist painters, they were out of his orbit. Events that had artificially aged him had also knocked awry the continuity of his own memories. It seemed a long time ago, if not in another planet, that he himself had been a child. Fathering none, and, in fact, acquainted with few young parents, Jed didn't know any children, as friends. He would have mentioned 'a bunch of kids' as he would comment on a 'flock of chickens' or a 'hill of ants'. He didn't individualize them. He simply had no truck with them.

This little girl, with her dark eyes in an angular face, wasn't a pretty little girl. Too thin. Too solemn.

Nell was in a crouch, leaning on her arms. 'Get back in there,' she said viciously.

'I want . . .'

Nell went across the bed on her knees. 'Go on. Get back in there and go to sleep.' Her fingers clawed the little shoulders.

Nobody spoke to Bunny O. Jones in such a fashion. Nobody came crawling at her like a big angry crab. Nobody

44

handled her so cruelly. Bunny was severely startled. She began to cry.

'And shut up!' said Nell.

'Yours?' said Jed coolly.

'She's not mine,' said Nell angrily. 'She belongs to the Joneses.'

'Oh . . . your niece?'

Nell laughed.

'You've got my mommy's things on,' wailed Bunny.

'Shut – '

'Just a minute.' Jed rose. Glass in hand, he came toward them. He was very tall next to Bunny O. Jones. He had no instinct to bend down. 'What's your name?' He felt awkward, speaking to this mite, and was impelled to speak loudly as one does to a foreigner or someone who may not readily understand the language.

'I'm Bunny O. Jones.' She twisted in Nell's harsh hands.

'Let go of her, Nell. Bunny *Jones*, eh? This isn't your aunt, is it?'

'What are you asking *her* for? She's not supposed to be in *here* . . .'

'Suppose you shut up a minute,' Jed said.

'She's my sitter,' sobbed Bunny.

'Oh, for Lord's sake.' Jed put his glass down and settled his jacket around him with angry shoulder movements. Now he knew what he had got into.

Nell's hands were off the child but not far off. 'I don't like you,' sobbed Bunny.

'I don't like you either, you damn little snoop.' Nell said.

One did *not* speak to these strange little creatures in such terms. Jed felt this much out for himself. It came slowly to him with a sense of how big he was, how big and how powerful even Nell was, and how helpless was the child.

He said, 'Nobody's going to hurt you, Bunny. Don't cry.'

But she kept on crying. Perhaps she didn't believe him. He couldn't blame her for that. She was shrinking away from Nell. And Nell contrived to loom closer and closer, so that the child was menaced and pursued and sought to escape, although the chase was neither swift nor far, but done in tiny pulses of the foot on the carpet.

'Why don't you ask her what she wanted?' Jed said.

'She wanted to snoop,' said Nell.

But it was clear to Jed that the little girl hadn't snooped for snooping's sake. It was clear to him that she had done nothing in malice. He put his arm like a bar across Nell's path and her throat came against it. 'No,' he insisted. 'There was something. What was it, hm? Bunny? What did you want?'

'It's too hot,' wept Bunny. 'I want my radiator off.'

'You might have asked,' Jed said scornfully to Nell. 'It's simple enough. I'll take care of it.'

He strode through the communicating door, which for all his caution he had not noticed to be open. The other room was stuffy. He found a valve. He thought, Towers, fold your tent. He noticed the exit to the corridor from here, from 809, and the key in the lock.

But the crying child, the girl again pursuing her in that gliding stepless way, were in the room with him.

'It's O.K. now,' Jed said. 'Cool off in a minute. Better get back to bed.'

'*She'll* get back to bed.'

Bunny broke and ran. She rolled into the bedclothes. She burrowed as if to hide. She was still crying.

Jed stalked into 807, making directly for the bottle. He had a notion to leave without breaking his stride, snatch the glass, drain it, pick up the bottle, cross the room, and fade away. But he was angry. What a stinking evening! First one thing and then another! Cutting phrases came to his mind. *Now* he understood that crack about fifty cents an hour . . . this late! . . . when it should have informed him, before, if he'd had the wits. He was furious for having been stupid. He was embarrassed and humiliated. He was even half angry with the little girl for having walked in and stared at Towers making a jackass of himself. A baby-sitter!

He wanted this Nell to know he was angry. So he freshened from the bottle the drink in the glass.

As Nell, on his heels, entered 807 and closed the door

firmly behind her, he snarled, 'Were you going to pay me my two bits an hour? Or wasn't this a fifty-fifty proposition?'

'What?' She spoke as if she'd been preoccupied, as if she hadn't quite heard. Her face was serene. She drifted toward the mirror. She touched her hair. It was as if, now that the door was closed, it might as well never have opened.

But Bunny was crying bitterly beyond the wall.

Jed said, furiously, 'Why didn't you tell me there was a kid in there?'

'I didn't know she was going to come in here,' Nell said.

Jed looked at her. For the first time, something nudged him, something said the word inside his head. But he didn't believe it. The word is easy to say. It falls off the tongue. But it is not so easy to believe, soberly, in all reality.

She walked to where he stood, by the desk that had become the bar.

He'd had cats press themselves around his shoes and ankles.

Nell fitted herself into the hollow of his shoulder and turned up her blind face. She was back where she'd been when so rudely interrupted. She was waiting for them to take up where they had left off. Jed stood still, angry enough to throw her brutally away from him, but bitter enough to stand still in unresponsive contempt.

The little kid was crying, in there, a tearing, breaking – a terrible sound.

Nell's tawny head rested against him. He grabbed her shoulder. 'Don't you hear that? You got something the matter with your ears?' He shook her.

'Hmmmmmmm?' She was smiling. She enjoyed being shaken. So he let her go. Her eyes opened. 'I heard you. I know what you said. You're mad at me. I don't see why you're mad at me, John. Johnee! I haven't done anything.'

'You haven't done anything?'

'No.'

'Well,' Jed said. He put the stopper in the bottle of liquor and kept it in his hand. He was ready to go. He could make no sense here, no use arguing, no point to that.

'Don't go,' Nell said rather shrilly. 'I haven't done anything. It's all right now, isn't it? She's gone.'

'Gone!' The sound of the child, crying in the next room, was preying on Jed's nerve-ends. As bad, he thought, as if a cat had been yowling under his window and he trying to sleep. It was too irregular even to be a background noise. It pierced. It carried you with it into its anguish. 'Can't you hear that!'

'That? She'll go to sleep.'

'She will?'

Nell shrugged. Using one hand, she lapped the long silk robe so that it didn't drag. She whirled, seeming quite gay. 'Can't I have another drink?'

The sounds the kid was making were not, Jed discovered, quite like a cat crying. Either a cat shut up, or it went elsewhere, or you went elsewhere. You got away. And if the cat cried where you couldn't hear it, why, let it cry. He didn't know anything about kids. But you didn't need to know anything. Just listening told you. *This* sound of *this* crying had to stop.

'Does it bother you?' the girl said rather casually, holding out her glass.

'It bothers the hell out of me,' Jed said roughly. 'She's scared. And you did that. Why did you have to jump at her like a wildcat? This the way you always treat your customers?' He poured whisky into her glass, hardly aware he was doing so.

She looked sullen. 'I didn't mean to scare her.'

'She startled *me*. O.K. But you knew she was in there. You're supposed to be taking care of her, aren't you? Listen . . .'

He was listening, himself, all the time. The sound was intolerable. 'You better get her to stop that.'

'When she gets tired . . .'

'You want the whole hotel up here?' he snapped.

'No.' She looked alarmed.

'Then do something. I'm telling you.'

He stalked toward an ash tray, walking between the beds. 'If I go in there, you'll sneak out,' Nell said flatly. The thought was crossing Jed's mind as she spoke. He put the whisky down beside the phone. He took his hand off the bottle as if it were hot.

'I don't have to sneak out, you know,' he said cuttingly. 'I can walk out, just about any time. I won't stay here and listen to that, I'll tell you.'

'If she stops crying, will you stay?'

'I doubt it.'

She put her glass in her left hand and worked her right as if it were stiff and cold. Her blue eyes had too much blue.

'This is no business of mine, remember,' Jed said, slashing the air with a flat hand. 'Nothing to do with me. But I'm telling you . . . Why don't you try being a little bit nice?'

'Nice?'

'Don't smirk at *me*. Nice to the kid in there. Are you stupid? What am I wasting my – '

'This is a date, isn't it?' she began. 'You asked me – '

But Jed was thinking how that little throat must ache. His own throat felt raw. He growled, 'Get her quiet. Get her happy. Go on.'

'If I do?'

'If you do,' he said rather desperately, 'well . . . maybe we can have a quiet little drink before I go.'

The girl turned, put down her glass, went to the door and opened it quietly. She moved obediently. She vanished in the darkness.

'I'm afraid,' Lyn said, 'Mr Towers must have gone out again. His room doesn't answer.'

'I can only say I didn't see him, Miss.' The man behind the desk at the Majestic wasn't terribly interested.

'But you did see him come in a little while ago?'

'Yes, I did.' He threw her a mildly irritated glance.

'Well . . .' she turned uncertainly.

'A message?' he suggested politely. She was a cute girl, trim and cuddly in the bright blue coat with the big brass buttons. And she seemed distressed.

'Yes, I could leave a note.'

He used a pencil to point the way to a writing-desk in the lobby, aiming it between a pillar and a palm.

'Yes, I see. Thank you.' Lyn sat down at the desk, put her purse down under her left forearm. She shifted the chair slightly so that she could keep an eye on a spot anyone entering the Hotel Majestic from the street must pass.

She thought he must have gone out again, perhaps through the bar. She hoped he wasn't, even now, upsetting her family. She herself didn't dare call home to ask. If they didn't know she was alone, so much the better. They'd have a fit, she thought. A fit. But . . . never mind. If they were anxious, too bad, but she was actually safe enough and they'd forgive and perhaps they'd even have confidence enough in her not to worry too much.

This was something she had to work out for herself. The family tended to side too blindly with her. Any man, they would assume, so benighted as to quarrel with their darling would never be worth her efforts to patch it up.

But I can be wrong, she thought, not far from tears.

No, she couldn't go home quite yet. She'd stay free for a while, even as long as a date might have lasted. Because this was important. She knew. It would be hard to explain how and why . . . embarrassing . . . maybe impossible. She had to work it out alone.

Anyhow, she didn't think Jed would go to her apartment. It would be capitulation. He wasn't that type. He was pretty proud.

Was she the type, then, to hang around? All right, she thought stubbornly, I *won't* be the huffy female type who, right or wrong, sits and waits for the male to come with his hat in his hand, like the dopey heroines of old romances who huffed and waited their lives away.

Ah, nobody was a type! This was Jed and Lyn, and this had to be worked out on the basis that they were unique and alive, and it had to be worked out *now*. To-morrow, the plane . . .

Wherever he was, he'd come back here. He hadn't checked out. It was all so childish . . . She could at least say that much.

'Dear Jed,' she wrote. 'It was all so childish . . .' She

watched a man and a woman cross the lobby. 'And I don't
want you to go West thinking that I . . .'

Am I doing this, she wondered, because I'm vain? 'Thinking
that I . . .' what? How could such bitter words have been
spoken between them? Because she'd been riding a high
romantic crest of expectation and been dragged rudely off it?
Maybe, for him, there'd never been such a crest. No, no.
That was a huffy-type thought, a fear to *seem* vain. She *had*
known that Jed was fond of her. She'd had *reason* to expect
him to say so or say more. Never mind that inside-out kind
of vanity.

She tore up the sheet and wrote again, 'Dear Jed: I've been
trying to find you because – ' A tear fell and the ink blurred
and she thought, Oh, no . . . not this! Wouldn't he be amused!

Would he? Lyn sat a long time with her hands quiet on
the desk. She worked it out. It was true. She was in love with
Jed Towers . . . in love enough to lash out at him, to get as
mad as that, to have it matter.

It was true. She had thought he might ask her to marry
him to-night. They'd been together, together . . . until that
old man touched this off.

And it was true. She'd have said yes. Gladly, yes. Yes, right
or wrong. Yes, just because of his mouth, maybe.

And they had quarrelled.

But it was *not* true that she thought him a cheap cynic. He
was . . . wary. Yes, he was. And he talked cynically. Part of
it was simple reporting – what he saw around him. Part of
it was defensive . . . or something like that. But it was talk.
People don't always know what they are. They talk *at* themselves a lot. She thought, but I can really be tough. If I believe,
then I must do . . . or all *I* said was only talk.

So Lyn worked it out, painfully. It was also true, whoever
began it, whatever it amounted to, she had been the one to
walk away, and cut off communication, and she didn't (she'd
always *said*) believe in that.

Very well. She clasped her hands. It was important. Here
was a crest from which she would coast away all her life
long. And a huff wouldn't do.

But what could she put on a piece of paper? If only he'd

come. People crossed the lobby, none of them he. To-morrow, that plane . . . Maybe he'd call her. No, it went so early. She could ask in the note. All her thoughts were splintering. Dawn was such a chilly time.

She took up the pen. 'Dear Jed: I can't let you go – ' But you can't keep him, Lyn. He isn't that type. Maybe he was only something charming and exciting flashing through your life, and what you seemed in his, for a little while, you'll never know. Might have discovered whether there was any meaning but not now – too late. 'Misunderstanding,' she wrote desperately. It was too late. She ought to go home.

What can I say? she wondered. What can I do? How can I go home?

Get out of here, Towers. Get out, quick. And forget it. Skip it. Jed paid his inner talk to himself no heed. He sat down on a bed. Under the verbalized thought ran uneasy pictures. What if the child were to cry a long time, and he, in his own room, could hear? How was he in a position to be the indignant guest, to protest, to do anything about it? *He'd* been stupid. Nell, the baby-sitter, had already made a complete jackass out of Towers. This rose to word level. He looked into his glass and contemplated this state of affairs.

When Nell came back carrying the child, he knew her reason. She didn't trust him not to sneak away. He remained quietly where he was. He was not entirely displeased. He wanted to watch her quiet the child.

'If you're scared, that's silly. Nothing to be scared about,' Nell said impatiently. 'Now don't start to cry any more. Shall I read another story?'

'No,' said Bunny. She wasn't quite crying at the moment, but she was shaken by an aftermath of shuddering. It was a reaction not subject to her control.

Nell set her down on her bare feet. Three strangely assorted people looked rather helplessly at each other.

'You know, *you* nearly scared the life out of me,' Jed said to the child in a friendly tone. 'And Nell, too. That's why Nell was cross.'

'She was . . . too . . . cross,' said Bunny as well as she could.

'That she was,' he agreed grimly.

Nell looked as if she would flare up defensively, but she did not. 'You O.K. now?' Her voice was edgy. 'You're not going to cry any more?'

Bunny wasn't sure enough to say. Her eyes turned from one to the other.

'I'm a friend of Nell's, stopped by to see her a minute,' Jed said, feeling his face flush. Why he should be trying to explain himself to this half-pint creature he didn't quite know. 'You ought to be asleep, I guess,' he went on awkwardly. 'How old are you?'

'Nine.'

Nine. What was it to be nine? Jed couldn't remember. The drinks were beginning to blur his concern a little. He began to feel these events less shattering, as if his ego went somewhere and lay down.

'I'm too hot,' said Bunny. 'I'm all sticky.'

'Come over here, then.' Nell went to the windows. 'We'll let some cool air blow on you. Then you'll be cooler. Then you can go back to sleep.' She nodded wisely. She pulled up the blind. She pushed up the sash.

Jed jumped quickly out of the line of vision through those windows. His back felt for the headboard. He poured another drink. The ice was all the way over there. So, no ice. Because he wouldn't cross in front of the windows. Place like a goldfish bowl. He knew. And that was where you made your mistake, Towers.

'See the lady, Bunny?'

Sob and shudder answered.

'I see a man, down there. He's playing cards.'

Jed's warm drink was nauseating.

'I think,' Nell went on, 'there's a kitten under the table.'

'What,' sob, 'table?'

'Down there. The card table.'

'I don't see . . .'

'Maybe it isn't a kitten. But it looks like a kitten.'

'I've got a cat,' Bunny said. 'Is the kitten strippe-ed?'

'No.'

'Is it grey?'

'Maybe.'

Miss Eva Ballew wrote, on the Hotel Majestic stationery, in her flowing script . . . 'seems to be a child crying in this hotel and I am so distracted, I hope you can understand what I am writing, since I seem to have two predicates and no subject in my previous sentence! My dear, this trip has really . . .'

Her pen paused. The child had stopped crying. Thank goodness, thought Miss Ballew. But now the night seemed hollow. She ducked her head enough to glance briefly out, under her blind.

The pen resumed, 'been a treat for all us teachers to have visited so many historical sites here in the East . . .' It was not a sentence.

She put down her pen suddenly and ducked again to look out, across the dark well of the inner court.

'I don't see any kitten,' Bunny said, 'at all.' Her pigtails hung down in front, swinging.

'Well, you're not looking . . .' Nell said softly. 'But you won't cry any more, will you?'

Jed glanced across at the bowl of ice. He rose. Why did she have to put the damn blind up? Dare he cross over? *Was* there anybody taking all this in? He'd just as soon get out of here without some guest having seen . . .

When he turned his head over his shoulder, the question dropped out of his mind. He stood quite still, puzzling about what was wrong. It seemed to him, definitely, that something was wrong. Bunny was kneeling on that radiator top. And Nell sat there, beside her. Nell's hand was flat on the little rump in the pink sprigged muslin –

Her hand was flat!

And there was some wild throbbing in this room.

Miss Eva Ballew, peering out, exclaimed. Nobody heard her, for she was alone. 'No!' she said. Then, whimpering, 'Oh, no! Please!'

The back of Jed's neck prickled. Must be his own pulse,

doing that throbbing. Just the same, it was intolerable. He began to move, silently, with the speed and grace of the young and strong.

'Way down under the table?' Bunny asked.

'Way down . . .' crooned Nell. 'Way, way down. Are you going to be quiet, I wonder?'

Bunny screamed.

Jed, with his finger tight around the little brown ankle, caught her forward pitch with one arm and said, on a rush of breath, 'Excuse me. Shouldn't lean out like that, for Lord's sakes. I *had* to grab.'

Nell's face turned, tipped back and up. She looked drowsy and unstartled. 'What?' she murmured. 'What's the matter?'

Jed had the child. 'Better come away,' he said to her. 'You'll catch cold, anyhow.' He could feel little twitches the whole length of the arm that held Bunny. He squeezed her as gently as he could manage. 'I'm sorry, honey, if I scared you. Trouble is, you scared *me* again. Sure did. Awful long ways down – kind of tough landing.'

Bunny, having screamed once in her surprise, did not begin to cry. Her face was pale. Her big dark eyes seemed to turn and keep some wisdom of her own.

Jed said, 'You're chilly. You're shivering. Aren't you sleepy now?'

Bunny nodded. She wiggled out of his arm. Her feet hit the carpet. She looked at him gravely. 'I can go to bed myself,' said Bunny O. Jones.

.

Miss Ballew straightened her cramped body. Her heart still lurched with that old devil of hers, that hair-trigger onset of the physical sickness of fear. She felt her throbbing throat. But what was going *on*, over there? Her pale lips tightened. She'd heard the man say, 'Put that blind down!'

So, it was to be secret, and it was male, and it was, perhaps, evil? She focused on her letter. 'And even in this wicked city,' her pen wrote, at last, too shakily.

'Put that blind down!'

Nell was still sitting by the window, still looking dreamy.

She stretched to obey and Jed thought there was something snakelike in the smooth uncoiling of her arching back and her reaching arm.

He stood at the door of 809, through which Bunny had marched herself. 809 was quiet . . . dim and quiet in there. So he closed the door, gently.

Bunny's rigid neck muscles let go a little. The head began to dent the pillow. The eyes were wide open. The hand reached for the little stuffed dog and tucked it under the stiff chin. The throat moved, against the fluffy toy, in a great and difficult swallow.

Jed swung around. You're nuts, Towers, he said to himself, angrily, using the words, in his mind, to knock out the pictures. You must be nuts. Where'd you get such a nutty idea? Nobody shoves kids out of eighth-storey windows, so they won't cry any more! Made his hair curl, the mere idea, even now. Where had he got it?

He began to fish ice out of the bowl.

It crossed the level of his mind where slang was not the language that there is something wild about total immersion in the present tense. What if the restraint of the future didn't exist? What if you never said to yourself, 'I'd better not. I'll be in trouble if I do?' You'd be wild, all right. Capricious, unpredictable . . . absolutely wild.

He looked at the girl. She was leaning beside him, watching the ice chunk into her glass, with a look of placid pleasure. She glanced up. 'You've had more than me,' she stated.

'That's right,' Jed said. He felt perfectly sober. The slight buzz was gone. He didn't bother to put ice into his own glass, after all. He wasn't going to have any more liquor, not for a while.

He gave her the drink. He sat down, nursing his warm glass.

He couldn't get rid of the shimmer on his nerves of narrowly missed horror. Nuts, Towers. Forget it. She was careless. Nobody's going to have an idea like that one. She just wasn't thinking what she was doing.

'I guess I wasn't thinking,' Nell said, with a delicate shrug.

'Are you a mind reader?' He sagged back on his elbow. 'That's a couple of times you've said what I had in my mouth, practically.'

She didn't answer.

'But you sure should have put a good hitch on the seat of her pants or something. Don't you know that's dangerous?' If the future didn't operate in your thinking, you wouldn't even know that word, he thought. Danger wouldn't have a meaning. Would it? He shivered. His mind veered.

If there *was* such a thing as telepathy, why, it would work both ways. If she could catch an idea out of his mind, then he might catch one of hers. Couldn't he? *Hadn't he?* Listen, Towers, don't be any nuttier than you have to be! Mind reading, yet! Fold your tent . . . fade away.

But he was hunting for comfort. He remembered something. He said, 'So you couldn't go dancing with me on account of the kid?' (So, you did feel responsible?)

'Uncle Eddie's on the elevator.'

'Huh?'

'He'd have caught me, going out,' she said placidly. 'He never lets me.'

'Your Uncle? Uncle Eddie runs an elevator? In this hotel?'

'Yes.'

'Oh,' Jed turned this information over. 'Maybe he got you the job, eh?'

'Yeah,' she said with weary scorn, 'my wonderful job.'

'You don't like it?'

'What's there to like?' she said. And he saw the answer come into her head. He saw it! He *read* it! There's you, though, Nell was thinking.

He closed his eyes and shook his own head. None of that. But he considered, and on the whole he thought he felt relieved. The future tense had operated. Hadn't it? If she thought ahead of her, to Eddie on the elevator?

His mind skipped to his own future. To-morrow morning on the aeroplane. By to-morrow night, a continent away, looking back on a weird evening, which was about over, he judged. Time to go.

His anger was gone. *He* was operating in the future tense, looking back, saying to somebody. 'And *what* a sitter! What a dame she turned out to be! Nutty as a fruitcake!' he would say. If he ever said anything.

'Well,' he spoke. 'Nell, I'll tell you. It might have been fun. We'll never know. So here's to the evening. Bottoms up and then good-bye. See you in South America, sometime?'

He grinned. Her eyes were too blue, not in the quality of the blue, but in the quantity. Strange eyes . . .

'You're not going,' she said, with no rising inflection at all. It wasn't even a protest. She just said this, as if it were so.

CHAPTER 8

The unwritten law that links green peas to roast chicken had not been flouted to-night. Peter pointed with his fork and winked. He wasn't really eating.

Ruth could eat no more than he. They picked and pretended. But nobody, she thought, was there for the sake of nourishment. The food marched by, as it were, in a sedate order, perfectly conventional, with no surprises, so that nothing about it should interrupt the real business of the banquet. Be seen, buzz, bow . . . Preen yourself, flatter your neighbour. Oh, it *was* fun!

But now they were nearly past the ice cream. They were at the coffee . . . the end of the line. Peter's conversation with his neighbours had been slowly lessening. Fewer and fewer words came out of him.

Ruth's nerves tightened right along with his. She let a little ice cream melt in her dry mouth. Peter was taking tiny sips of water, oftener now.

Every once in a while, the buzzing and the bending-to-chat got a little unreal for Ruth – whenever Bunny came into her mind. It was a little distressing that her vision of Bunny in her bed was shaky and unreal, too. Bunny, she told herself, making words, as if the words had power, was sound asleep. As sound asleep as if she were in her bed at home. Oh, Bunny was real! Warm and beloved, Bunny was there. But those hotel rooms, those formulas, did not wrap her around with the safe sense of being home.

But *of course not!* Ruth said to herself.

Still, it was a great city, vast and unknown, and the West Side seemed divorced from the East Side, where they were . . . seemed far.

'I'd like to call back to the hotel pretty soon,' she murmured to Peter. 'Where are the phones?'

'Saw them as we came through,' Peter said. 'Around the corner, past those mirrors . . .' He dabbled in his ice cream. The toast-master was still chatting peacefully.

'Have I time, do you think?' breathed Ruth. They, at the speaker's table, were as far as it was possible to be, away from the double doors to the mirrored place beyond which were the telephones. Parade, in my pink, thought Ruth. Conspicuous. Peter could not go, *now*.

The toastmaster shifted in his chair. He sipped his coffee. Ruth felt all Peter's muscles wince. For the toastmaster glanced their way and made a tiny nod. His eyes nodded deeper than his head did.

Imperceptibly, Peter responded. The toastmaster shoved with his hips and his chair began to move backward.

Not now! No time, now! Ruth would call, afterward. After the man had said whatever he was going to say. Later than that, for without intermission, it would then be Peter's turn!

It would be good to call, later, with this tension gone. And all clear. Oh yes, it would be much better.

There was no doubt that Bunny was sound asleep, anyway. Ruth must now lift her chin and turn her head and listen sweetly to the Speaker of the Evening. (Oh, what was he going to say! Oh, *Peter!*)

Bunny was nine and surely had fallen sound asleep by this time.

The toastmaster rose like Fate. Ruth released her glass and patted her cold hands together in tune with the crowd. 'I am happy,' the man said, 'to be here . . .' Who cares how happy they are? Always so *happy!* She could hear every tiny wheeze of the toastmaster's breathing. Peter had turned slightly in his chair, as if this were fascinating, but no concern of his, of course. . . .

'And I am particularly glad,' the man said, 'to have this opportunity . . .' They were always so *glad!*

Ruth smiled faintly and let her fingers play with her water glass. She must display the perfect confidence she felt, that under her pounding heart lay so truly sure. . . .

Jed fended her off and it was balm to do so. It was sweet revenge on the whole female race who had loused up his evening. He laughed at her. He had her by the elbows, at arm's length. 'It's not that automatic, toots,' he said. 'I know. There's a school of thought that says it is. But make a note, why don't you? There is such a thing as being choosy.'

Her rage made him laugh and he let himself go back against the headboard. 'The time, the place, and the girl,' he mocked. '*I'll* choose them all, and this ain't *any* of them, sweetheart.'

She looked ready to screech. But then her face closed down, took on that sleepy look. She leaned heavily on his grasp, limply now, with nothing but her weight.

'So I'll say so long, Nell,' he snapped, watching her suspiciously. 'Understand?'

The wild thing about her which, he knew now, had attracted him in the first place, and then made him uneasy, was getting entangled with her will. She wasn't sleepy. Oh, no! Now, he knew that the dreamy look was, on her, a dangerous sign. Maybe a part of her did go to sleep. Maybe it was the part that took into account the future.

He sat up, thrusting her with stiff forearms. He was a little bit sorry for having indulged himself in that laughter. He wondered just how he was going to get out of here without a row, without, say, too much racket. He said, quietly, 'I'm really sorry, but I've got to go. Some other time, Nell.'

She didn't seem to hear. Then, she did seem to hear, not his voice, but something less loud and less near. Her pupils travelled to the right corners of her eyes.

He heard it, too. There came a discreet tapping on the door of Room 807.

Oh-oh! Exit Towers! Jed muttered under his breath, 'I'll get out the other way, through the kid's room.'

'No.' She spoke no louder than he, not a whisper, only a movement of the lips that was nearly mute. 'You won't.' The words were clear and stubborn on her small mouth.

' . . . find me,' he said in the same fashion, 'you'll lose your job.'

The tapping was gently repeated. It would persist, insist. It was patient.

Nell's face lit in malice and delight. 'No, no. I'll say . . . you pushed in here. Say you're . . . after me.'

Jed's eyes flickered. She would, too. She damn well would! He was quite sure she would. For the hell of it! For the sheer wild mischief of it! And, if she did, the benefit of the doubt rests with the female.

'You wait,' she said. 'I know who it is.'

Their almost soundless conversation was taking place in a depth of silence that was uncanny. The room pressed silence around them. The city bayed at the feet of the building, but here, high, they spoke without voices in a soundless place. Although someone kept tapping in gentle hope upon the door.

'Who?' Jed was rigid in alarm. How in hell was he going to get off this spot? What to do?

'It's Uncle Eddie, I can get rid of him.'

'I can get out,' Jed gestured. His eyes were sombre.

'No.' She knew her wild will held him.

'What, then?' He ground his teeth.

'In there. Be quiet.' She intended him to hide in the bathroom!

He rose, slowly, letting her go. He could knock her aside. He could get swiftly into the kid's room.

And she could yell.

And she was opening her mouth.

Jed stalled, by picking up the bottle and hiding it in his pocket. Quickly, she put his glass into his hand. And then she had him by the elbow. She was pushing, guiding.

The tapping faltered. 'Nell?' someone said softly and a trifle anxiously. 'Nell?'

Nell said, 'Who's there?' Her very voice seemed to stretch and yawn. But her eye was watching Jed and her face rippled. She would just as leave cause trouble . . . just as leave as not!

'It's Uncle Ed. You all right?'

Nell's brows spoke to Jed. Twitted him with it. *Well?* they asked, *Am I?*

He growled, voice muted in the bottom of his throat. 'O.K. Make it snappy.' He went into the bathroom and pushed the door back behind him, not quite tight.

'Gee, I'm sorry, Uncle Eddie. I guess I must have been asleep,' he heard her saying . . . heard her yawning it.

Towers stood in the bathroom and cursed Towers in his mind. What'd she have, a hex on him? Of all the damned lousy situations. He looked at his watch. He said to himself, Let Uncle Eddie get away and I am gone. Brother, will I be gone. I really fade. Without a word, he'd go. Without a waste motion.

You picked up dames, sure. Every once in a while. On a train. Maybe in a bar. Sometimes a thing like that turned out not bad. If it was sour, you blew. In cold blood. You got out, fast.

How come Towers was hiding behind a door?

He sat on the edge of the tub, to wait, reciting curses, rehearsing in his mind his swift passage out and away.

Lyn turned away from the phones. No answer.

I will smoke another cigarette, one more. I will wait until ten more people come in from the street, ten more. I can write a better letter. I know I can. I can try.

CHAPTER 9

Eddie looked at his niece in negligee and his eyes were disappointed. He said, 'I brought the cokes.' Disappointment made his voice bleak. He had the bottles in his hands and he went toward the desk and stood there looking down at the tray, the bowl of melting ice, and Nell's glass. 'What's this?' An inch and a half of rye and ginger ale remained in the glass.

Nell said, 'You were a long time, Uncle Eddie. I got thirsty. Let me wash that out.' She took the glass out of his meek hand. 'I ordered ginger ale,' she said defiantly to his troubled eyes. 'Mrs Jones said I could.'

'That was nice of her,' said Eddie.

'Want a piece of candy?' Nell said brightly over her shoulder. 'She said I could help myself.'

'I don't believe I care for any,' Eddie said. 'Thanks.' His bleak stare went around the room.

Nell pushed in the bathroom door. She went to the wash basin and rinsed the glass.

Not even in the mirror did her eye meet Jed's. There was not a gesture, not a wink, not a sign that she even knew he was there. Jed felt his blood rage. It was an abuse of power. A little grin, a tiny glance, a hint that they conspired to fool this Eddie, would have eased the thing, somehow. But, oh, no! She'd forced him into the ignominy and now she let him stew in it. He could have beaten her. He ground his teeth. Some baby-sitter!

Eddie said, 'Little girl sleeping? I see you closed her door.'

Nell left the bathroom, pulling its door behind her. She

64

would have closed that, but Jed threw his strength on the inner knob and they tugged secretly, silently, and she lost.

'Could you hear if she cried or anything?' Eddie was saying in worried tones.

'The light bothered her,' Nell lied calmly.

'Now she's sleeping, though, it won't bother her.' Eddie, gentle on the knob, released the catch. 'I think Mrs Jones would rather it was a little bit open, Nell.'

'O.K.,' she said indifferently. She waited for the coke.

'And it's getting later. It would be better if you took Mrs Jones's clothes off, Nell. Honest, I thought . . .' Eddie's adam's apple betrayed his hurt, although his voice was careful.

'Gee, I meant to.' Nell's fine teeth bit her lip. 'I was so kinda comfortable . . . I just didn't hurry . . .'

At once, Eddie brightened. 'Sure you meant to, Nell. I know that. Uh – ' he fiddled with an opener. 'Why don't you do it now, though?'

'All right, Uncle Eddie.' She sat docilely down on the little bench and slipped her feet out of the mules. Eddie scrambled for her own black pumps and she put them on. Then she took the earrings off, slowly. She put them into the jewel box. Her fingers began to pick up other things, tidying them, putting them away.

Eddie brightened with his lightening heart. 'That's right! Good girl!'

She turned her bent head, smiled at him. She rose and her hands worked at the sash of Ruth's gown. Eddie's eyes turned primly down. Nell said, sounding modest and shy, 'I'll just step into the closet.'

Her Uncle Eddie took a long relieved pull on his coke bottle.

She came out of the closet in her own rumpled dark dress. It had been a heap on the closet floor for some time. But now Nell made elaborate motions of finicky care as she hung the negligee on a hanger and arranged its folds. 'There,' she said, 'that's just the way it was. Is that O.K., Uncle Eddie?'

He beamed on her. 'That's fine, Nell. Now!' He sighed.

'Mightn't be so very long before they get back, you know. But you're all set.'

'We'd better drink our cokes,' she said mildly. 'It might look better if I was alone in here. Do you think?'

'You're right,' he said. 'Yes, you're right. I told them I was going to drop in, but it *would* be better if they find everything quiet and you on the job, eh? Well, here you are. You know,' he blurted, 'I want to do everything *for* you, don't you, Nell? You know why I want you to take a nice little job like this. I want you to get started.'

'I know, Uncle Eddie.' She was all meekness. Her lashes were lowered. She showed no sign of impatience at all.

He took a swig. 'Well, it's because I believe in you, Nell. And Aunt Marie does, too.' His blink was contradicting the courage in his voice. 'I think you'd rather be here with us than back in Indiana.'

'Oh, I would,' she murmured.

'If the insurance company would have paid on the house and furniture – but as it is, there's nothing left. You know that. So you'd be on some kind of charity, till you got a job, and I wouldn't like that for Denny's girl.'

'No,' she said.

'You know I haven't got much money,' he went on. 'I got a steady job. But you can see why it's a good thing if you can . . . kinda get over this trouble pretty soon.'

'I'm O.K.,' she said without force.

'You're *better*. That's sure. You certainly are a lot better.'

She was looking at him with that blind blue abstraction she sometimes had. 'But they ought to pay,' she said. 'Why can't we make them pay?'

'I don't know how we can,' said Eddie uneasily. 'I don't know if we can ever *make* them. You see, they claim, because the fire was *set* . . .'

'It was an accident.' Her voice went higher. And he cleared his throat nervously. '*Wasn't* it?'

'It was. It was. That's what they said in the court, yes. It was an accident.'

Suddenly her face was calm, her glance cold. 'So why don't they pay?'

'Well, the insurance company, they figure – I tell you, Nell. I think it's best to kinda forget about that. Might take a lawyer and quite a lot of money and you wouldn't be sure you could win, you see? I think the best thing is, forget about that and try and get started . . . There wasn't so much insurance. How's the coke?'

'It's good,' she said meekly. 'Is yours?'

'Fine.' He took another swig. It might have been wine, for he seemed to mellow. 'You just needed somebody to stand back of you,' he said. 'Me and Marie knew that, Nell, at the time. And we do stand back of you. We really do. *I* can understand just why it is you get kinda restless streaks. *I* don't blame you.'

'You've been good, Uncle Eddie.' Her lips barely moved.

But he looked very happy. 'It's just that I can see how it is,' he said eagerly. 'After such a terrible experience, a lot of little things seem pretty *little*. Don't matter much, eh? That's the way it is, isn't it, Nell?' The little man seemed to hold his breath. Every fibre of his worried little being was yearning to make contact, to understand and be understood.

The girl didn't look up, but she nodded.

He swallowed and leaned closer. He said softly, 'You want to remember, Nell, your father and mother don't blame you. You mustn't ever think that they would. They know you wouldn't ever have done anything bad, Nell . . . not to them. You see, wherever they are, *they* must know that even better than we do. And if they could talk to you . . .'

'I don't want to think about them,' she said in a perfect monotone. 'I don't want to think about them.'

'No, no,' said Eddie quickly. 'Nobody wants to make you think . . . about that. But I been trying to tell you one thing, Nell. The doctor said it would be good if you'd know . . . and here we're so quiet and all, maybe I can say it. Me and your Aunt Marie, we stand back of you. We believe in you. We don't doubt, for one minute, you set the fire walking in your sleep that night . . .'

He watched her face. Her lashes flickered. 'That's what the court said,' she remarked lightly.

'But – but – don't cry,' he whispered to the tearless blue of her eyes.

'I'm not going to cry, Uncle Eddie.' She turned her empty glass in her fingers. She put it down.

Eddie blinked the tears out of his own eyes. He swallowed the sick flutter of his heart. That Julie his brother married, something about her he never had liked. But surely she'd never been mean to Nell. Denny wouldn't have stood for it. Denny wouldn't be mean to anybody. No, no. There could be *no reason*. She was still shocked, poor Nell. She *couldn't* cry. She *loved* them. She'd meant no harm. She'd cry, some day. *Sure*, she'd cry.

'Tasted pretty good, didn't it?' he said cheerily.

Jed controlled his rage almost immediately. He'd got into this jam by getting senselessly angry and it was about time, he told himself, that Towers used the brains he was born with. He settled coldly to wait this out. He could hear their voices and a part of his brain recorded the words.

But, in part and at the same time, he was reviewing the way he had come. It had come back to him, the year he was nine. Not the events of that year, so much, as the feel of it. By then, he mused, the boy was all adjusted to the family. He had been trained. He knew what the rules of conduct were in so far as his mother and father had taught them. All that was smooth, so smooth he couldn't remember much about it.

But he was also stepping out, newly bold, into the world his parents did not know. He was beginning to test himself more daringly with his contemporaries. School, the gang, society and his personal meeting with it had been the part of life that was filled with interest. Warm security at home and one toe in the cold waters of the outer world, testing to take his weight.

Pretty soon, he remembered, the boy began to pick up the stuff that isn't down in the home rules. The ways and the means, the manoeuvrings, the politics, the exchanges of influences, the worming one's way, the self-interest of every-body and how to use *this* for himself. Through high school and a part of college, and then the war, and the final bitter tutoring of the peace. Sharper lessons, all the time. Trial and error. What worked and what didn't. Lessons in the possible. Knocking home what's possible and what is not, and what is only a fool's goal.

So now, here's Towers. A young man, out to 'make his fortune' as they used to say in the old stories when he was nine. Out to make his fortune without a dream in his eye. Wangled himself a damn good job on the coast. Pulled strings to get it. Young man on the way up, and gangway for him! Old enough to begin to think, if only obliquely, that he might take a wife.

So Lyn was on his mind, eh? A dream, there? He pushed her image away.

So here was Towers, skipping the whole middle of the country, to-morrow, letting it flow under his plane, not planning to stop and see the family. Why? Oh, business, he'd said. They understood. Not wishing to stop and hear the blind love speaking, pretending he was nine?

Well, he thought, people probably settled on a pattern that worked, for them, and there they stayed. And if his pattern was shaping up a little differently, why, no use arguing. Dad talked service. Lived it, too, as far as anyone could see. And it worked, for him. Or anyhow, it worked pretty well. It made a kind of guide, a touchstone . . . Jed could see. And mother talked love – *was* love, dammit. He wished, a little wistfully, that the world really was what they seemed, incomprehensibly, able to assume it was. How come they could hang on to that kind of peace, whatever it was, and make it a shell around them?

Or did they? Were they besieged by disappointments? Were they only huddled in their shell, like people in a fort? He didn't see much of them, these days. It was the family tradition to exchange only cheerful news, as far as one could. Did their hearts despair?

He didn't want to think so. He supposed you battled through, sooner or later, and came out on the other side of struggle, when you accepted something or other and put the blinders on and just kept them on and didn't look, any more.

But when you're young and scrambling in the market-place, you have to watch out. Yeah, out. Not in. That is, take a hard look at the way the world operates. You didn't want to be pushed around.

Oh, Towers was a wise one, all right, sitting on the bathtub, behind the door. He knew the score.

His jaw was tight. Definitely, a detour, this little expedition. Get on your way, Towers!

Still talking, this Uncle Eddie? Still yammering in there?

'And so, I thought,' Eddie was saying, 'the best idea is for you to start out easy. Take a little job once in a while. The thing is, Nell,' he was expounding his creed, 'you do something for somebody else and you do a good job. So they're glad to pay you for it. Then you're earning. You're being useful. You got to get into the idea. After a while, you'll get so you can do a bigger job or a better job. You'll get into the idea. You'll get over being so restless.'

'You told me all this,' she said. Her ankle was swinging.

Eddie saw it and silenced himself.

'Going?' she murmured. Her head fell against the chair. She turned her cheek. Her eyes closed.

'I'll take the coke bottles. I don't think the Joneses are going to be so long now. Couple of hours, maybe. Tired?'

She didn't answer. Eddie rose and the bottles clinked together as he gathered them. She was breathing slowly. 'I'll be in the building,' he murmured. His eye checked over the room. Everything was in pretty good order. Looked all right. He took up the glass from which Nell had sipped her coke.

Absorbed in his own thoughts, his anxieties, his endeavours, his gains and his losses, Eddie went mechanically toward the running water, which was in the bathroom.

CHAPTER 10

Even before he met, in the mirror, the little man's shocked and unbelieving eyes, an appraisal of this new situation flooded clearly through Jed's thoughts. The jig was up, all right. O.K. He rose smoothly. The frightened eyes followed him up, still by way of the glass. But Jed was smiling.

This could be handled.

The mind has an odd ability to play back, like a tape recorder, things heard and yet not quite attended to at the time. Jed knew, immediately, that Eddie could be handled. And that it was a way out for Towers, too.

He knew from what he had overheard that Eddie was by no means sure of his little niece Nell. Eddie had stuck his neck out, getting her this job. Eddie knew she was unreliable, to put it mildly, although he tried, he struggled, to make himself believe everything was going to be all right. All that pitch about his belief and understanding, all that stuff, was a hope and a prayer, not any conviction. Oh yes. Eddie had taken an awful chance here and Eddie was liable.

All Jed needed to do was use Eddie's self-interest. Very simple. Jed would apologize. Nothing happened, really. Had a couple of drinks, very sorry, sir, he'd say. I'll be leaving now. No harm done and enough said. Nobody need say anything more about it.

Jed would make it easy for the other fellow. He'd ask silence as a favour to himself. Eddie could escape by magnanimity the consequences of his own folly. Eddie would be glad to say 'good-bye' and only good-bye.

So long, Nell, Jed would say, quietly. And he'd be out of it.

So Jed rose, smiling, knowing he had the power of charm and attractive friendliness when he chose to use it. In the time it took him to rise and open his mouth, the little man had jerked with a mouse-squeak and backed toward the door, keeping a frightened face toward Jed's tall figure in the tile-lined gloom. Jed, not to alarm him, stood quietly where he was.

But Nell, like a cat, was lithe lightning across room 807. She had the standing ash-tray, the heavy thing, in her wild hands. She swung it up. Jed's lunge and Jed's upraised arm missed the down-swing. The thing cracked on Eddie's skull. The detachable portion of heavy glass clanged and boomed and echoed on the tile. And Jed said something hoarse and furious and snatched the thing out of her hands cruelly, and Nell jabbered some shrill syllables.

All at once, the noise was frightful.

Only Eddie made no noise. He sank down, very quietly.

There was an instant when everything was suspended. Then the phone began to ring, in 807, and at the same time Bunny's voice screamed terror, in 809. And the glass part of the ash tray, rolling off a brief balance, rumbled and at last stopped rolling, unbroken.

'Now!' said Jed thickly. 'Now, you . . .' He squatted beside the crumpled little body.

Nell turned and walked over to the telephone, which in some freak of time had rung four times already.

'Hello?' Her voice was fuzzy and foggy.

Jed touched Eddie's temple and then his throat.

'Oh yes, Mrs Jones,' Nell said. 'I guess I must have been dozing.'

There was a pulse under Jed's fingers and he stopped holding his breath.

'She's fast asleep,' Nell said, blithely. (And Bunny kept screaming.) 'Oh, no, no trouble at all. Everything's just fine.'

Jed, crouching, found himself listening to that voice. It was pretty cool. Just the faintest undertone of excitement. It could pass for enthusiasm. He could feel the child's cries pierce him, and he shuddered. He looked down at Eddie, feeling a blank dismay.

'Yes, she did. Went right to sleep after her story, Mrs Jones. I hope you are having a nice time.'

Phone to ear, Nell pivoted to see what Jed was doing and one stare was as blank as another. Her hand rose to hover over the mouthpiece.

The kid was frantic in there! Frantic!

'Please don't feel you need to hurry, Mrs Jones,' purred Nell, 'because I don't mind – What?'

Her eyes widened as her voice acted surprise. 'Noise? Oh, I guess you can hear the sirens down in the street.' Her hand clamped on the mouthpiece. She said, through careful fingers, 'They're just going by. There isn't any fire near here.' She laughed. 'Oh no. You just have a real good time,' she advised gaily. She hung up the phone.

Her face set.

'It's a wonder he's not dead,' Jed growled. 'You little fool!'

'Isn't he?' said Nell absentmindedly.

She walked into 809.

Jed's hand, going about the business with no conscious command from his numb brain, felt Eddie's head carefully. The dry hair crisped on his finger-tips. He left the dismayed welter of his thoughts to pay attention, here. Couldn't tell what the damage was, but there was, at least, no bleeding. Gently, he straightened the body. He lifted it, shifting it all the way over the threshold within the bathroom and, reaching for the thick bath-mat, he slid it gently between the hard tile floor and the head. He took a towel and wet it. He washed the forehead gently, the eyes, and the cheeks.

Eddie's breathing seemed all right . . . a little difficult, not very. Jed thought the pulse was fairly steady. Knocked out, of course, but perhaps . . .

He lifted his own head suddenly.

Bunny was not screaming. The empty air pulsed in the sudden absence of that terrible sound.

Jed sat motionless on his heels. A trickle of sweat cut a cold thread of sensation down his neck and blurred in the fabric of his collar.

Ruth stepped with slow grace out of the phone booth. 'Have a real good time.' The phrase rang in her ears. Not the *mot juste* for such a night as this! This Night of Triumph! A time to keep in the mind for reference, forever. Even now, so soon afterward, it was an hour to live over again, and feel the heart stop, when Peter got up from his chair, and lurch, when he began, so nervously. And pound proudly, because she soon knew that all these politely listening people were warming to the man, who began a little bit nervously and shyly, as if to say, 'Gosh, who am I?'

And then, Peter getting interested, himself, in what he was saying. Everybody feeling that. First, the words, coming out grammatically, properly placed, in full sentences. Then, the thought transcending, and driving the grammar into vivid astonishing phrases that rang just right. And finally Peter in the full power of his gift, taking directly from his mind and heart the things he knew and believed. The heads turning because they could not help it. They must hear this.

He was still excited (oh, bless Peter!) and he was reaping his reward. Now that his speech was over, now that they were pushing the tables out of the middle of the floor, and music was playing, and people stood in little groups, and he in the middle of the largest group of all.

Peter was reaping an evening's-worth of praise and glory. But maybe even more. Maybe even the real thing! Was it possible, the Joneses wondered, that some might remember, might retain and refer to some small part, at least, of what he had told them?

A victory! But the rehashing, the reaping, the wonderful fun of this, might go on for hours.

Ruth turned her bright nails into her palms. Bunny was fast asleep. The girl had told her so. Everything was fine. The girl had said so.

But Ruth stood, trembling, in the hall of mirrors, and she knew in her bones that everything was *not* fine.

'Don't be silly!' she gasped to her own image. 'Don't be such a *mother!* Don't spoil it, now!'

Peter's head craned toward her out of the group, and she gave him a gay little signal of the hand that meant 'all's well'.

For it must be so.

But that hadn't sounded like the same girl. Oh, it was the same voice. But it was not the same manner. The girl on the phone, just now, was neither dull nor passive. *She wasn't stupid enough!* No, she'd been too decisive. Too . . . too darned *gay!* Too patronizing . . . 'Run along, little Mrs Jones, and have your real good time. Don't bother me.'

'Don't you be so *silly!*' Ruth told herself once more. 'Are you going to be mean and spoil Peter's wonderful night, being such a hick and such a female? What's *wrong* with you?'

She shook herself and walked forward.

'What's wrong, oh, what's wrong where Bunny is?' her bones kept asking.

Peter was in full flight, amplifying something he hadn't touched on quite enough in the speech. Men, standing around him, were smoking with very deliberate and judicious gestures, and nodding, and breaking in to quote themselves. 'As I said at lunch the other day . . .' 'I was saying to Joe . . .' It seemed as if only last week or the other day they'd been thinking the same things Peter thought. They'd been telling somebody, in some fumbling fashion, that which Peter has just told them so well. (Ah, sweet praise!)

'O.K. hon?' Peter was tuned in on the wavelength of Ruth's bones. Often and often he'd heard what they were muttering. But now, when she answered, smiling, 'All quiet. Everything fine, Nell says,' Peter didn't hear her bones proclaim, 'But I don't believe it.'

'Good.' He squeezed her, swung her, 'Ruth, this is Mr Evans, and Mr Childs, and Mr Cunningham.'

'How de do . . . how de do . . .'

'Husband of yours has a head on his shoulders and a tongue in his head, Mrs O. – uh – Mrs Jones. Fine talk. Fine.'

'I thought so, too,' said Ruth in sweet accord.

'Isabel, come here. Turn around, want you to meet . . .' The women murmured.

Peter said, 'So, a man says to you, "Honesty is the best policy." You don't need to look up his antecedents, and if you find his great uncle stole fifty cents thirty years ago, figure what he *says* must therefore be suspect. What he *says* you can agree to or *not* agree to. However, if he claims he is pro-honesty, but expects you to rob a bank with him, you can see the difference, I hope. In fact, you had better learn the difference.'

'Right,' said a cigar.

'I claim the truth can come out of a rascal's mouth, but how can a rascal fool us, if we learn to sort out words from deeds and keep our heads clear?.'

'Just what I said to Isabel. I said . . .'

'And how old is your little girl, Mrs O. – uh – Mrs Jones?' Isabel was cooing.

'Bunny is nine.'

'Ah, I remember Sue when she was nine,' said the woman sentimentally. 'A sweet age. A darling year.'

Ruth smiled, bright-eyed. She had no voice for an answer.

CHAPTER 11

Mrs Parthenia Williams said, 'I can't help it.'

'Aw, Ma,' her son said, keeping his voice down in the evening hush of the place where they stood. 'Listen to me – '

'I can't help it, Joseph, hear?'

For old Mr and Mrs O'Hara in the front suite, the Hotel Majestic had somehow, in the inertia of the years, acquired the attributes of home. Now Mrs O'Hara wasn't very well. She wasn't ill enough to warrant a nurse, yet they were unwilling to risk her being alone. So Mrs Parthenia Williams came by day and sometimes, when Mr O'Hara had to be away, she remained late into the evening. Whenever she did so, her son, Joseph, came to see her home.

As they stood in the hush of the eighth-floor corridor, Joseph said, 'You better keep out of it, Ma. You know that. Don't you?' He was a thin nervous Negro with an aquiline face.

'I know what I know,' his mother said.

Mrs Williams's chocolate-coloured face was designed for smiling, in the very architecture of her full cheeks, the curl of her generous mouth, the light of her wide-set eyes. Nothing repressed her. Nothing could stop her from saying 'good morning', in the elevators, in her beautiful soft voice. She seemed to acquire through her pores bits and scraps of knowledge about all these strangers, so that she would say, in the corridor, 'Did you enjoy the boat trip, ma'am? Oh, that's good!' with the temerity of an unquenchable kindness. Mrs

O'Hara, who was sixty-two and so often annoyingly dizzy, felt at rest on Parthenia's bosom. She told Mr O'Hara it was as if, after thirty orphaned years, and in her old age, she were mothered once more. (Mr O'Hara crossed his fingers and knocked on wood.)

Joseph knew his mother's ways and adored her, but some of her ways . . . He tried to protest this time. 'Some things you can't – Ma!'

'Something's scaring that baby in there nearly to death,' Parthenia said. 'She's just a bitty girl. She's in 809 and her folks next-door. I spoke to them to-day. A real nice child. And I can't help it, Joseph, so don't you talk to me.'

Her big feet carried her buxom body down the corridor. 'If her folks ain't there, somebody ought to be comforting her. It's not good for her to be so scared.'

'Ma, listen . . .'

'All right, Joseph. Her papa, he was asking about a sitter and I *know* they were planning to go out. Now, if her mama's there, that's one thing. But I got to ask. I can't help it. I don't care.'

Jed got to his feet. His eyes rolled toward the frosted bathroom window. He unlocked it and pushed it up. Cold air hit him in the face.

The deep court seemed quiet. He thrust his head through to look down into the chequered hollow. He couldn't, of course, see all the way to the bottom. He couldn't see Bunny's window, either, for it came on a line with this one.

He could see that old biddy across the way and she was walking. She walked to a chair and held to the back of it with both hands and let go with a push and walked away. And back again. He could see only the middle section of her body, and those agitated hands.

The fear that hadn't been verbalized, even in his mind, seeped away, and he wondered why he was looking out of the window. He wondered if the dame over there was upset because she had been hearing things. He wondered, and in the act of wondering, he *knew* that someone must have heard all that commotion.

Get out of here, Towers, he warned himself, while you got the chance, you damn fool! Before all hell's going to break loose. This guy's not going to die. He'll be O.K. He's resting peacefully. Look out for Towers!

Jed realized that he had a perfect chance, right now. While the wildcat was in 809, Towers could fade out of 807. And Towers would run like crazy away from here.

What he heard himself growling aloud, as he stepped over Eddie's body, was, 'What in hell is she *doing* in there!'

The knock made him jump. Too late! He groaned. He eyed the distance from where he stood to 809. Through there, where the key, he remembered, dangled its fibre tag on the inside of Bunny's door . . . that would have to be the way out, now that someone, and he didn't doubt it was trouble, knocked on 807. He waved. How would he get by whoever it was, once in the corridor? He would, he thought, get by and he'd better.

Then he saw Nell standing in the way. She looked at him and moved her left hand. It said, 'Be still.' Jed shook his head and tightened his muscles for the dash. But Nell was too swiftly across 807 . . . so swiftly that Jed caught himself and ducked backward into concealment again, only just as she opened the door to trouble.

'Yes?' Jed could see her and he cursed, silently, her dark-clad back (she'd changed her clothes!) and the fantastically cool lift of her chin.

He expected a man's voice, an official voice, cold and final. But the voice was deep music, and not a man's. 'I heard the little child crying so bad,' it said. 'Is there anything I can do?'

'Why, no,' said Nell in chill surprise.

'You taking care of the little girl for Miz Jones, ma-am?'

'Yes.'

'That's good. You know, I spoke to the little girl and her mama . . . she might know me. I wonder could I comfort her?'

'She's all right now.' Nell moved the door. But Parthenia's big foot was within the sill.

'I had so much experience with children. I get along with

children pretty well, it always seems. She was scared, poor child! I hear that.'

'Just a nightmare,' said Nell indifferently.

'Come on, Ma,' Joseph said. 'You asked. Now, come *on*.'

'Who are you?' said Nell sharply, peering at him.

'This is my middle boy,' Parthenia said with pride. 'I've got three boys and two girls. Yes, Ma'am, a big family but they raised. Hurts me to hear a baby cry so bad. Just hurts my heart like a pain. Poor little child . . . and all so strange . . .' It was like a song, a lullaby.

'It's none of your business that I can see,' said Nell coldly.

'Maybe not,' said Parthenia. But her big foot stayed where it was. A big foot, worn with carrying a big body, bunioned and raked over at the heel . . . a big strong stubborn foot. 'Maybe not,' the lovely voice said sadly, 'but I got to try to stop my pain. Can't help trying, ma'am, whatever child is crying.'

'She's not crying now,' said Nell irritably. 'And it's too bad you've got a pain. Please let me close this door, will you?'

'Ma – '

'You got a charm for the nightmare?' Parthenia asked with undefeated good-will.

'If you don't get out of here, I'll call somebody.'

'Ma . . . Excuse us, miss . . . Ma, come *away*.'

'I can't feel happy about it,' said Parthenia softly mournful. 'That's the truth, it's just,' her soft voice begged, 'could I be sure she ain't scared any more? Little children, being scared sometimes in the night, you got to be sure. Because it hurts their growing if they're not comforted.'

'She's comforted,' spat Nell. Then she changed. 'But thank you for asking,' she said in a sweet whine that had a threat to it, somehow. 'I guess you mean well. But I really can't ask you in here. I don't know who you are or this man – '

Joseph plucked his mother from the doorway roughly.

'Good night, then,' Parthenia said forlornly and, as Nell closed them out, 'If I was white I wouldn't – '

'Shush!' said her son. 'Hurry up. Get the elevator. Get home. She's trouble.'

'Trouble,' his mother murmured.

'You ought to know better, Ma. I told you. We can't fool around that white girl. Believe me, not *that* one!'

'I wasn't fooling. Something's bad wrong, Joseph. Baby's mother's not there. I can't feel happy about it.'

'Listen, Ma, you better feel happy because you can't win. You know that, don't you? You can't stick your nose in that white girl's affairs, if you're right a million times over.' He rang for the elevator, jittering.

'No child,' said Parthenia gravely, as they waited, 'no child gets off the nightmare as quick as that. No child, Joseph. Nobody's child.'

'You can't do anything, Ma. Forget it, can't you?'

The elevator stopped. The door slid. Parthenia's enormous foot hesitated. But she stepped in, at last, and Joseph sighed as they sank down.

He heard her mutter, 'No, I wouldn't go.'

'Shall we stop for a bite?' said he in nervous animation. 'You hungry, Ma?' She didn't answer. 'Ma?'

'I don't believe I'll stop, to-night, boy,' Parthenia said.

'Not hungry?' He grasped her arm and pushed her off the elevator, around the bend, to the back way out.

Parthenia said, looking at the stars, 'No, I'd make a fuss. I wouldn't go.'

CHAPTER 12

' . . . Niggers!' said Nell.

All of a sudden, all Jed's cool purpose to depart was burned up in the flame of his raging need to tell her off.

'You damn wildcat! Dope! Fool! What's the idea of doing what you did? What's the idea of swatting him down like that? What in hell did you think you were doing? What kind of cockeyed dream was in your stupid brain? Answer me!'

He shook her. The dark dress was too short. Also, it was cut to fit a more matronly body. So she looked younger and less sophisticated, but also older and dowdier. Her head went back on her neck, as a snake's head poises to strike, and her tiny mouth over the sharp tiny chin looked venomous. Her face with the yellowish glow to the unlined skin was no age one could guess or imagine.

'Answer me!'

She was angry. 'What's the matter with you?' she cried. 'You didn't want to be seen, did you? Did you?'

He could see her pupils, pin-points in the fields of blue.

'You're the one who's a dope!' cried Nell. 'You didn't want him to see you? Well? He was walking right in there.'

'So you'd just as leave murder the man, eh? Just for walking? So you don't care whether he lives or dies? Do you?'

'He's not going to die,' she said scornfully. 'I didn't hit him so hard.'

'The hell you didn't. You hit him as hard as you damn well could. Just luck that you didn't . . .'

82

'Did you want to be seen?' she hissed.

'So you did *me* a favour? Don't do me no more.' He flung her to one side of him, holding both her wrists in one hand. It crossed his mind that time was sifting by. It began to look as if no one had sounded any alarm to authority. Nothing was happening. He yanked her along as he went to peer through the window-blinds.

The dame across the court was just standing there. He could see her hands on the back of that chair.

He swung Nell back into the centre of the room. She stumbled, unresisting, although she looked a little sullen. She said, 'I thought you didn't want to be seen in here. You acted like it.'

He looked at her. 'Just a point,' he said dryly. 'The little man had a perfect right to walk in there if he wanted to. He wasn't doing a thing he shouldn't do.' Nothing happened to her face, no change of expression. He might as well have said it in Choctaw, or something. 'Didn't think of that, eh? I suppose,' he mocked, 'you "just weren't thinking"?'

'I thought you didn't want him to see you.'

'So you shut his eyes. That's logical. That's great!' Jed wanted to slap her, hit her, worse than he had ever wanted to hit anything smaller than he was. He took his hands off her as if she would soil them. 'O.K. Where did it get you? What did it do for you?'

She didn't seem to follow.

'I was going. Remember? I'm still going. I'm going faster and farther, if that's possible. And don't think you can frame me with any lying yarn,' he stormed. 'I'll be gone,' he snapped his fingers, 'like smoke! You don't know who I am, my name, where I came from, or where I'm going to be. And you'll never see me again in this world, Nelly girl. The point I'm trying to make. You might as well . . . might a hell of a letter better . . . have let your Uncle Eddie show me out! Do you get that? Can you?'

She said nothing. But she moved a little bit, working around, he thought, to put herself between him and the door. He laughed. 'Single track, your mind. One-idea-Nell. One at a time is all you can handle? Listen, you never had a chance to keep me here since I found out you were a baby-sitter. Never. Not a chance. All your monkeyshines . . .'

'Why not?' she said.

'Say I'm allergic,' said Jed shortly, 'and skip it. I've got nothing against kids.' His hand chopped the air nervously. 'That's got nothing to do with it. They let me alone, I let them alone. Nothing to me.' He didn't like this line. He shifted, quickly. 'Start thinking about yourself, and think fast, Nell. How *you're* going to get out of the jam you got yourself into, I couldn't say.'

'I'll get out of it,' she murmured carelessly.

He didn't hear. He was listening for something else. 'It's quiet in there,' he muttered.

'She's all right,' said Nell, carelessly. Her lids seemed to swell at the outsides of her eyes, puffing drowsily.

'What did you tell her?'

'I told her nothing to be scared of. Somebody just fell down.' Suddenly Nell laughed, showing her teeth. 'Somebody *did*,' she giggled.

'How true,' said Jed thoughtfully. His anger churned inside him still, but he had the upper hand of it. He had an uneasy feeling that he had better not indulge in so simple a response. He stepped around one of the beds and looked into the bathroom. 'Eddie's going to be missed, you know. Naturally, you didn't think of that.'

'He won't be missed,' she said indifferently. 'He's off duty.' She sat down and put her ankles together and looked at her feet. Her toes made a miniature sashay.

Eddie was about the same, still out, breathing better. Jed turned around.

Nell fell back on her elbows, smiling up. 'Take me dancing?' she said coquettishly. 'Johnee?'

'Dancing!' he exploded.

'Uncle Eddie's not on the elevator now.' She seemed to think she was explaining something!

He wanted to say, I'd just as soon take a cobra dancing. But he said, 'And? Who sits with the baby, in the meantime?'

'It's a dumb job,' she said. 'I don't like it.'

His lips parted, closed, parted. He sat down, facing her. It seemed important to make plain what it was she left out of her calculations. It seemed important to try reason out against unreason. It seemed necessary to try to cut through a wall of fog, to clear things up.

'You're in a mess,' he said, rather patiently. 'Don't you know that?'

'What mess?' She was sulky.

'You bop this guy, this Uncle Eddie. O.K. Now, what's going to happen? Look ahead a little bit. The Joneses come home from the party. There's a body in the bathroom. What are you going to say?'

'It's only Uncle Eddie,' she murmured.

Jed took his head in his hands. He meant to make a semi-humorous exaggeration of the gesture, but it fooled him. He was holding his head for real.

'Now, listen carefully,' he said. 'What's *going* to happen? Future tense. Consequences. You ever heard of them?'

She used a word that rocked him with the unexpectedness of its vulgarity. ' – , Uncle Eddie isn't going to say it was *me* who hit him.'

He had to admit that he himself had reasoned along this line. For a moment, he was stopped. 'O.K.,' he resumed patiently. 'So Eddie won't tell on you. Then what *is* the story? Did he knock himself out? What did knock him out? Who? Don't you see, you've got to have an answer?'

'I can say you did it,' she answered placidly.

'*After I'm gone*, you'll say it!' He was furious.

'Unless we're out dancing.'

He stood up. This time he spat it out of his mouth. 'I'd just as soon take a cobra dancing as you.'

'You asked me when you first – '

'*Then*,' he snapped. 'That was before I knew what I was getting into. Now I see you do the way you do, I retract, believe me.' He paced. 'Why don't you *think*, first! That's what I can't understand. You swat him down without a brain in your head working. Can't you imagine what's *going* to happen? Doesn't that mean anything to you? Ever plan? Ever figure ahead? What's wrong with you, anyhow? How come you do the way you do?' He looked coldly down. 'I think you're insane.'

It's easy to say. The words fall off the tongue. This was the first time Jed had ever said it, in perfect sincerity. He did think she was insane.

She lifted her head, on the neck, slowly. It was the neck that lifted, as if it uncoiled. She said a few ugly words. Then she was screeching and clawing at him and biting his self-defending hands with savage teeth and her shrill refrain was, 'No, I'm not! No, I'm not! Take it back! You take it back!'

He handled her, but it wasn't easy. He got her in a locking hold and he shut her mouth with his hand. 'Cut it out! Cut it! You'll scare the kid. You'll have cops in here.'

She was still screeching, as well as she could, 'Take it back!'

'O.K. O.K. I take it back. If that does you any good. So you're a model of foresight and wisdom. So anything! So cut it out!'

She cut it out. She seemed satisfied. It was necessary to her that the word not be used. The word 'insane'. But it was a matter of words. The words, 'I take it back' were just as potent. Which, thought Jed grimly, is insane.

He felt chilled. He did not want this to be true. She was a crazy kid, a wild kid, in the slang sense. Only in the vernacular. She was all mixed up and she didn't know how to stop and think. He told himself that was it. But he felt sad and chilly. He didn't know what to do. She was limp in his hold. Then he knew she was not so limp, but too happy to be held so tightly.

He loosed her, warily. He said, vaguely, 'Why should we fight? Makes too much noise.' He listened. There was no sound from the child's room and he let out his breath. 'Good thing, *she* didn't begin to howl again. I can't take any more of that.'

Nell said, 'I know.' A flicker of contempt crossed her face. 'I understand about the future,' she muttered.

'I talk too much, sometimes.' He was trying to be careful. 'What I need . . . Finish the bottle with me?' He took it out of his pocket. 'Good thing this didn't get smashed in the excitement.' He looked vaguely around. 'Aw, what's a glass?' He tipped the bottle.

She took it from him with both hands. The notion of drinking out of the bottle seemed to tickle her.

He said, 'Say, where did the Joneses go?'

'Why?' Her voice was as careless as his.

'I was wondering how late — Was it theatre? Or a party someplace?' He feigned relaxing.

She still had the bottle in both hands. Carrying it, she walked between the beds and sat down near the head of one of them. 'I don't know,' she said vaguely.

'Shindig, eh? That sounds like a party. Somebody's apartment?'

'Your turn.' She gave him the bottle. Her face was full of mischief. She said, 'I understand about the future, Johnee. Everybody does.'

'I guess so,' Jed said.

She took a slip of paper off the table between the beds, where the phone was. She began to pleat it in her fingers.

'You think I'm stupid?' she asked, looking sidewise.

'Everybody's stupid, sometimes. Looks kinda stupid of the Joneses not to say where they'd go. What if the kid got sick or something?'

'Oh?' Nell said brightly. 'You mean they should have thought ahead? About the future?'

'Did I say something about the future, ever?' He grinned. He was thinking, I got under her skin, though. Must have. He felt better.

Nell tore the paper idly into fancy bits. When Jed passed over the bottle she let the bits fall on the carpet. Too late, Jed saw them fall. He received, in a telepathic flash, the news. What had been on the paper. Why she had torn it. How she had foxed him. And the news of her sly laughter.

He was chagrined. He kept himself from showing it, he hoped, and from anger. They may know at the desk downstairs, he comforted himself, where the kid's foks went. He said, and perhaps this was the result of the damped-down anger, 'Say, what was this about a fire?'

'Fire?' Nell smoothed the bedspread. She cocked her head.

She seemed willing to talk about fire if that's what he wanted to talk about. It didn't mean anything to her.

'I got a little bit of what your Uncle Eddie was saying.'

'Oh, that.'

'Was it your house, burned? Your parents? I thought he said so.' She didn't answer. 'Upset you, Nell?'

'That's what they say,' she said demurely.

'Who?'

'Oh, doctors. Uncle Eddie. Aunt Marie.' She frowned. 'Aunt Marie went to the show to-night.'

'Where was the fire?'

'Home.'

'Some small town, was it?'

'It wasn't big.' She curled up her legs.

Small, all right, Jed thought to himself, if they let this one loose. But he said to himself, quickly, No, no, there must have been some testing. Yet his thoughts went sombrely on. Probably Eddie showed up ready and willing and anxious to take her far, far away. Probably the town would just as soon not face up to it. Nell wouldn't be any of the town's business, far, far away.

'So it was an accident,' he said, making a statement. 'Well, I'll tell you something. The future's one thing you got to look out for. The past is another. Because the past adds up. You know that?'

She frowned.

'This accident. Your father and mother both died in it?'

'It was an accident.' He heard the jump of her voice to a higher pitch. He knew it was a threat. It warned, Look out! It reminded him of that screeching tantrum. It warned, Be careful! Danger! Touchy!

'Well, I'll tell you,' he drawled, nevertheless, 'and it's a funny thing. You take one accident, why, that's too bad. Everybody's sorry. Poor Nell.' She was curled up as tense as a coiled spring. He tried to fix her gaze, but it was all blueness. He kept on drawling, 'But you take *two* accidents, that's different. That's not the same. It's really funny how, after a second accident, right away, the first accident doesn't look so much *like* an accident, any more.'

Her face went blank, either because he'd hit her with an idea, or she didn't know what he was talking about.

'Good thing to keep in mind,' he said lazily.

She said, 'They didn't do anything to me.' Her face was sullen. But Jed felt a sick wave of absolute knowledge.

He watched her. He said, as quietly and steadily as he could, 'What I'm saying ... the first time is different. But things like that have a way of piling up. It gets harder. Because it counts. It adds. One and one make more than two. They make questions. So, maybe you better not get walking in your sleep,' he finished gently.

She didn't move. He thought, *I got it over*.

And the bottle was empty. He gathered himself to get up, now, and go quietly.

Miss Eva Ballew believed in many things. One of them was duty. She walked toward the telephone. One of them was justice. She walked back to the chair.

But however strong her beliefs and her conscience, Miss Ballew was a physical coward and knew it and all her life had fought her weakness. Now, she realized full well that she had been prodded too many times ... three times ... and she was taking too long ... much, much too long ... to make up her mind what she ought to do.

Sometimes, if you take time to decide, the need to do anything passes of itself. Miss Ballew reproached herself with bitter shame and she walked toward the phone.

But ...

She walked to the chair, she banged her fist on the chair back and the pain helped her. Justice. Very well. If justice won, it was because this was going to take more physical courage, and she was a coward, and she wished to deny her cowardice.

She went to the dresser and got her purse, not to be naked without it, once away from her room. She left the room and, flogging herself, marched around the hollow square of the eighth floor.

Nell hadn't moved. Jed, all the way up, standing, said, 'So

long.' He felt a little pulse of compassion for her, who was lost, and had no inner compass to find the way again. 'Be seeing you.'

Once more, and briskly, somebody's knuckles knocked on 807's door.

Nell was up, lynx-eyed.

'Oh no,' said Jed softly. 'Oh no, my lady, not again. Not this time!'

He faded. Towers faded, the way he had to go, through the door to the kid's room, to 809 . . . and closed it behind him.

CHAPTER 13

Miss Ballew rapped again. Because she was afraid, she did her best to be angry. She knew someone was in there. Did they think they could lie low?

The door opened so swiftly it surprised her. A girl in a dark dress, not a very big girl, not very old, looked at her with blue, blue eyes and said, with an effect of stormy anger, although her voice was low, 'What do you want?'

'My name is Eva Ballew. My room is across the court on this floor.' Miss Ballew's words were as neat and orderly as herself. She tended to begin at the beginning.

'Yes.' The girl seemed to listen, but not to hear, almost as if she was listening for something else. And it seemed to Miss Ballew that her anger was aimed elsewhere, also.

'Before I call the manager of this hotel,' said Miss Ballew more boldly, to command attention, 'I think it only fair to ask whether you can explain.'

'Explain what?'

'What is going on in these rooms,' said Miss Ballew, loudly and firmly.

'I don't know what you mean.' The girl was looking at the caller, but not seeing her, almost, thought Miss Ballew, as if she were *also* looking for something else out here in this bare corridor.

'There is a child,' said Miss Ballew coldly. 'Is she your child?'

'I'm taking care of her.'

91

'I see.' Miss Ballew's mouth was grim. 'Yes, so I imagined. Is there or was there a man in here?'

'A man?'

Miss Ballew longed to cry, Pay attention, please? 'I saw the man,' she announced, sharply, 'so that is an unnecessary question and you need not answer it.' She could see into room 807 and no one else was visible, at least. She did not feel physically afraid of rather a small girl. And if the man had gone – Miss Ballew was encouraged. She said, yielding to curiosity. 'Who was the man?'

'Listen, you can't – '

'The child,' cut in Miss Ballew coolly, 'has been crying in a most distressing manner, twice. And I have witnessed certain rather strange scenes over here. I must ask for an explanation.'

'Who are you?' began Nell.

'I am someone who will call downstairs if I do not get the explanation,' said Miss Ballew dictatorially. 'In the first place,' she went on, beginning at the beginning in her orderly fashion, 'a while ago, you were at the window with the child?'

'Yes, yes,' said Nell impatiently, 'what are you trying to – '

'I have already told you. I am trying to find out whether or not it is my duty to call the manager.'

'But why should you?' Nell stepped closer, with the door behind her now. Her glance slipped down the corridor to the right, briefly.

'Because,' snapped Miss Ballew, wishing this girl would pay attention and not carry on this duel with some invisible thing, 'it seemed to me, for one thing, that the little girl very nearly fell out of the window.'

'Well, she didn't,' said Nell carelessly. 'While you were at your snooping you must have noticed that.'

Miss Ballew bridled but stood her ground. 'Snooping or not, I wish to see the child.'

'See her?' For the first time, Miss Ballew felt that her words were heeded.

'Yes, see her for myself.'

'You've got a crust!'

'Nevertheless, if I do *not* see her, I intend to call the authorities.' So much for rudeness, Miss Ballew's eyebrows remarked.

'I don't know what's the *matter!*' Nell said in whining exasperation. 'What do you want to see her for? She's sleeping. What are you talking about?'

'Why did she scream so dreadfully?' Miss Ballew narrowed her eyes.

'When?'

'The second time. Come now, stop evading, young woman.'

'What?'

'I think you'd better let me in.'

'*You* listen,' Nell said. 'I'm here to take care of her. You're a stranger. How can I let a stranger in? How do I know . . .'

'You don't,' agreed Miss Ballew, 'but unless I see her for myself, the manager or the detective here *must*.'

'What business is it of yours? I don't underst – '

'Are you afraid to let me see her?'

'I'm not afraid,' said Nell shrilly. 'But I can't do it. I'm not supposed to. You talk about duty – '

'Now, see here. I am a schoolteacher. I'm sure I look like one. You ought to be able to tell that I am a responsible person.'

'You're trying to cause trouble.'

'On the contrary. I wish you would realize that I could have called downstairs directly. I felt, however, that it was not fair to cause trouble, as you say, if there is no reason. Therefore, I have taken the trouble to step around here. There may be some simple explanation and if the child is perfectly all right and asleep, then there is no occasion for any trouble at all. Now, is that clear?'

'What would her mother say if I let any old person?'

'What would her mother say about you entertaining a man?' In the same tone, Miss Ballew would have said 'about your smoking opium'.

'He's gone.' The girl's eyes flickered toward the right again. 'And she *is* perfectly all right. She *is* sleeping.'

93

'I beg your pardon if I seem to insist in the face of your direct statements, but after what I saw – '

'Saw?'

'Perhaps you don't know that the Venetian blind was so adjusted that I *could* see.'

'See where?' Nell's head went back on the neck.

'Into the child's room.'

'It's dark in there,' Nell said stupidly. Perhaps a little drowsily.

'Not quite. There was a very little light, perhaps through the connecting door.'

'Light?'

'And the child did stop her screaming rather abruptly,' said Miss Ballew.

Nell's eyes slipped sidewise. 'What did you see?' asked she.

Ruth was only half listening to the women's voices. She would have preferred to be in the group of men where the talk, she was sure, must have more meat in it. It could hardly have less. These women, from far-flung spots, had no basis for gossip and, since they weren't even sure who each other's husbands were (except Ruth's, of course) they didn't even have the fun of ranking each other.

Except Ruth. She could have been preening herself, for no woman had missed her rose-coloured presence at the Speaker's elbow. But her heart wasn't in it.

There was a faint superstitious element, too, a fear that if she got to thinking herself too darned smart, something bad could happen. She felt, absurdly or not, as if she rode the narrow edge of danger, as if, by standing here among these party-tainted women, she was taking a risk. She said, 'Yes, indeed,' again, and again the sense of danger fluttered her heart.

Peter strode out of his group and snatched her out of hers. Their steps fell together to the music as if they were at home at the Saturday night Neighbourly. 'Smatter, hon?'

Ruth looked up with clouded eyes. 'Now, I thought I had you fooled.'

'Nuh-uh. Worried? About Bun?'

'I'm sure I'm silly.'

'No, you're not sure,' he said. 'Something on the phone call bother you?'

'I don't know.' She slid her hand higher on his sleeve. 'Probably it's just because I'm a hick and this great big town scares me. Listen, Peter, even if I don't always act it, I am a grown woman. Let me do something. Let me take a cab over to the hotel and see. I'll be perfectly all right, and I'll come straight back and dance till dawn. And I won't *spoil* it.'

'We could leave now,' he said, guiding her in a turn.

'But . . . the fun!'

He grinned, admitting the fun. 'Man from Chicago, I'd like to have a few words – '

'Then do. Please. If you go, I'll feel terrible. *You* can't go.'

'My night to howl,' he grinned. 'Got cab fare?' He would let her go. Peter wouldn't *make* her spoil it.

'Not a penny,' she confessed.

He danced her into the mirrored exit, squeezed her, let her go, and gave her a five-dollar bill. 'Don't trust any handsome strangers with all this moolah on you, baby.'

'I won't.' Ruth thought, I don't trust that stranger, that girl. It's what's wrong with me.

She wouldn't let him come any farther than the cloakroom with her. He looked at her little watch from her bag and said rather seriously, 'It shouldn't take you long to get across town at this hour.'

Somebody said, 'Oh, Jones,' or was it, 'O'Jones'?

Ruth smiled at him. She left the scene. She felt, at once, much better to have escaped, to be free, to be going.

A doorman found her a cab. The city thought nothing of a young woman in evening clothes taking a cab alone in the night. No look. No comment. The city minded its business.

In the outer night, in the streets, were many many people, all minding their business. Millions and millions of people, thought Ruth, not only here, but millions of other places, too, who never heard and never will hear of me. She thought, For each of us, me, and every one of them, how few are anything but strangers.

CHAPTER 14

Jed stood in the dark. He heard Miss Ballew introduce herself and knew at once *this* was the old biddy from across the way. Through the slats of Bunny's blind he could see her room, still lit.

He wondered if he were going to be able to get around the two of them, out there, without an uproar. Maybe Nell would let her into 807. But if not . . . He wondered about going around the hollow square in the other direction. He had an impression that one could not. It was only a U after all. Suites across the front, perhaps. Dead ends for the corridors.

He wondered if he could take refuge by knocking at a stranger's door. God forbid, he thought piously. No more strange hotel rooms for Towers. Only God knew what's in them.

He rehearsed his exit in his mind.

And he meant exit. Total exit. There were worse things in the world than sitting the night out at the airport.

The stairs went down, he knew, just beyond the elevators. Well, he could move fast, Towers could, on his long legs. In his mind, he placed all the stuff in his room. Where to snatch up this and that. He travelled light. There was little to snatch. He could be in and out of that room, he thought, in a matter of sixty seconds, and exit, bag and baggage.

Then let her screech her lies.

He had little doubt she'd cook up some lies, all right. If necessary. Or even just if it seemed like fun at the moment. Or, if she was mad at him. And, he thought, she is!

Dancing, yet!

Unless he had knocked, with a few words in a few minutes, a totally unfamiliar idea of caution into her head. Of course, he'd been thinking of the kid. He'd been trying to get into Nell's head the danger, the undesirability, of harming the kid.

So that Towers could fade, of course.

Damn it, Towers had to get out of this! A fine mess! Assault, maybe, on account of Eddie in there, and the benefit of the doubt on Nell's side. For long enough to make it a mess, all right. And Eddie, tempted, if not almost obliged, to say something hit him but he doesn't know what. Everything just went black, and so forth. That would be the easiest thing for Eddie to say, wouldn't it? Eddie could even kid himself that it was true.

So there's Towers, in a jam. Jail, bail, telegrams. Would his high-powered new job, his big fat step in the up direction, wait quietly for some judge to let him loose? And would a judge?

Nuts! He ground his teeth. Trouble would breed trouble. He had to get out of here. Never *was* any business of his, the kid and the sitter. Not his kid, for Lord's sake. Strangers. All strangers. If the parents didn't know any better – Probably didn't give a damn what happened to the kid, he thought angrily. Off on a shindig, all dressed up. Probably drunk as skunks by now, and painting the town. Why should Towers care?

Why should he be so angry about it?

And also if Eddie, the elevator boy, stuck *his* neck out and got bashed in the head for it, what was that to Towers? He didn't feel for Eddie. Eddie had it coming.

He still stood, just inside room 809, still listening. He didn't know what he was waiting for. No question, really, but what Towers better move fast. That old biddy had her teeth in it now. Listen to her. 'I wish to see the child.' Icicles hanging off every word. Sounded like a pretty stubborn old dame. 'And she's white,' he thought, not quite letting himself know why the word came to him.

Nell was stalling, but he thought that the old biddy would

walk right over her. He took a soft step. He'd better get going.

Have to steam himself up to some fast footwork, now. Once out, out of this hotel, he thought, let them whistle for the wind! He'd fade. He was never here. He'd be clear away, on the town, one in millions. Gone, like smoke.

And Towers right back on the track again, on his way up, as he had it figured.

No one would ever know a thing about this. How would they? Why should they?

Kid was asleep and anyhow the old dame out there was going to raise a row. She was hell-bent to do it. No need for him to figure in it. Let her do it. She was the type to do it. Let it work out this way. Why should he duplicate what she was already going to do?

He might drop a word at the desk, on his way out, though. He could have heard a commotion over here, from his own room. The old biddy had, from hers. Just as well tip the hotel. Then Nell *couldn't* stall her.

His eyes had adjusted to the dark in here. He could see the far bed was undisturbed. On the other, the little kid must be asleep.

Funny thing she didn't wake up during his late wrestling match with the wildcat. It hadn't been a silent one.

That bed was awfully flat.

His hair moved with his scalp.

He crept a few steps in room 809. Of course, she was an awfully little girl, probably wouldn't make much of a hump on a bed. He didn't know. He'd – damn it – he'd hardly ever *seen* a sleeping child. He didn't know if they made a hump or not.

There wasn't any little girl on the bed.

He looked at the windows and Towers was sick and sickness was going through him like cream swirling down through a cup of coffee and something thumped on the floor.

He knelt in the dark crevice between the beds. He felt, blindly. Something threshed. He wanted light but he didn't dare. His fingers found a thin chilly little . . . what? Shoulder?

Yes, for he touched a soft braid. He felt for the face, the warm lips, and the breath, but touched, instead, fabric.

God damn her to hell, the God-damned bitch, she'd bound and gagged the little thing. Oh, damn and blast her rotten soul! Aw, the poor little . . .

'Bunny?' he whispered. 'Bunny Jones? Aw, Bunny, poor kid. Listen, sweetheart, I wouldn't hurt you for a million dollars.' His fingers verified. Yes, her ankles were tied together. Wrists, too. And that cruel – stocking, he guessed it was, in and over the mouth!

'You fall off the bed, honey? Aw, I'm sorry. I'm sorry about this. Mustn't make a noise, though.'

Oh, Lord, how would the child *not!* if he ungagged her. It was not possible for her not to cry! He knew this. It would not be in her control. She must cry out, must make sound as soon as she was able.

But she mustn't! Or Towers would never get away.

Now, what could he do? Thoughts flashed like frightened goldfish in the bowl of his brain.

Grab her, just as she was? Take her with him? Yeah, and run past the two women at the other door, with the kid slung over his shoulder. A kidnapper, yet!

Fantastic! No, no, better not do that.

He sat on his heels. His hand tried to comfort the little girl, smoothing her hair. He thought, coldly, 'So you're in a jam, Towers?'

But then his mind went all fluid again and in it those fish-flashes and in the panic he thought, Damn it, no! He thought, I've got to fix it for the kid and get out, too!

Look out for yourself, Towers! Nobody else will. It came back to him, in his own words. A guide, a touchstone.

All right! Use your head! Nothing was going to happen to the kid beyond what already had. The woman out there would keep Nell busy. And he, Jed, would tip off the hotel. So, for five minutes' difference, five minutes more . . .

Crouching near the floor, in the dark he could hear the city crying, its noise tossing and falling like foam on the sea, as restless, as indifferent, as varied, and as constant. And he saw himself, a chip, thrown, blown, attracted to another chip, to swirl, to separate, to grow arms and be, not a chip, but a swimmer, and push away.

Once away, who would know? Never see these strangers again.

Mess!

He leaned over and whispered, 'I'm afraid you'd cry if I undo your mouth, honey. I wouldn't blame you. I'm just afraid you can't help it. We can't make any noise, just yet. Listen, I'm going. Going to get somebody. Get your daddy.' His hand felt the leap of the little heart. 'Get your daddy,' he promised. 'Be still just a little while longer. It'll be O.K.' He didn't lift her to the bed for she was more hidden where she lay. 'I am a friend,' he said, absurdly, out of some pale memory in a boy's book.

He got up and went softly to the door of 809.

CHAPTER 15

'I saw,' said Miss Ballew in her precise fashion, 'the child, as I suppose, sitting up in the bed and a figure approach and appear to struggle with her. The cries then stopped, most abruptly. So you see, I require,' said she hastily, 'some explanation. I cannot believe,' she added vehemently to cover the shake that was developing in her voice, 'that any grown person would use force on a child. What, actually, were you doing?'

Nell looked sleepy.

'Answer me,' said Miss Ballew angrily. 'If it wasn't you, who was it?'

'You said you *saw* –' There was a hint of impudence in the girl's face, something saucy that must be crushed at once.

Miss Ballew said, coldly, 'I certainly did see *someone*, doing *something*, which has very much alarmed me. I would advise you, young woman, to take me to that child at once.' (But she was afraid again. She was dizzy with her fear.)

A door, to her left and the girl's right, opened and closed very fast. A man was in the corridor and had passed rapidly behind Miss Ballew almost before she could turn her head. Moving with long gliding steps, he rushed on, he vanished around the corner. Miss Ballew staggered in the wind of his passage.

It had been so swift, so startling, so furtive, and there had been a white roll of his eye.

'Who was that!' Her knees felt mushy.

The girl looked as if she could hop with rage, as if she would begin to bounce, like popcorn.

'Explain, at once!' cried Miss Ballew and reached out to shake this stupid creature.

The girl collapsed at her touch. 'Oh, oh,' she said. 'Oh – ' and bent her arm against the door-frame and buried her face in her arm. 'Oh, I was so scared! Oh, miss, whatever's your name. Oh, thank you! You've saved me!'

'What!'

'That . . . man!' said Nell, muffled.

'Why, he must have come out of the next – Yes, I see he did! Out of the child's room!'

'Yes. Yes,' cried Nell. 'Now do you see? He was in there all the time. He said if I didn't get rid of you . . . Oh!'

'Oh, dear,' said Miss Ballew faintly.

'He said he would – ' Nell's body pressed on the wood as if in anguish.

Miss Ballew rocked on her feet and reached for the wall.

'He just forced himself in here. He was so wild,' Nell cried, 'and strong!' Her face peeped, now, from the sheltering arm. 'I didn't know what to do!'

Silence beat in the corridor while Miss Ballew fought with her wish to fall down. One heard, one read, and all one's life one feared, but not often did one encounter . . . But the ruthless predatory male was, of course, axiomatic.

'There wasn't anything I could do.' The girl's whine broke the spell. 'I couldn't – I'm not very strong.'

'But he is getting away!' moaned Miss Ballew. For she heard, in the mists of her horrors, the yawn of the door to the fire stairs and the hish-hush of its closing. This, she felt, was outrageous. Outrageous! That such things . . . in a respectable hotel . . . and go unpunished! The anger was starch to her spine. She tightened her mouth, gathered her strength, and bustled past the girl into the room. She threw her stout sturdy form on the bed and reached for the telephone.

Downstairs, Rochelle Parker shifted the lifesaver expertly into the pouch of her cheek. 'Yes?'

'This is Miss Ballew,' said the agitated voice. 'I'm in room –
what?' she cried to the girl. 'What is this number?'

'Number 807,' said the girl quite promptly and calmly.

'Room 807. A man has just fled from here.'

'*What* did he do, madam?'

'Fled. Ran. He ran away.' Miss Ballew was often forced to
translate her remarks. 'He was up to no good.' She tried to
be basic. 'Get him!' cried Eva Ballew and reverted. 'He must
answer for it. He must face his accuser and be brought to
book. This is criminal and he must be apprehended.'

'Just a moment, *please*,' said Rochelle. She pressed the
button that would discreetly summon Pat Perrin to a phone.
Almost at once, she plugged him in.

'Yeah?'

'807's on, Pat.'

'Yeah, what is it?'

'There was a man in here,' said Miss Ballew. It was as if
she said 'African lion'. 'He is trying to get away, right now.'

'What did he look like?'

'What did he look like?' cried the teacher to the motionless
girl.

The girl's lips opened and her tongue slipped to moisten
them. 'He . . . had red hair.'

'Red hair!' Miss Ballew's voice both informed Perrin and
doubted the information, for this had not been her own
impression.

'Very dark red,' said Nell, 'brown eyes, freckles.'

'Dark red, brown eyes, freckles, and tall. I saw that. And
I think a grey suit.'

'Brownish,' Nell said, 'and a blue shirt.'

'Brownish? Well, some light colour. And a blue shirt. And
he took the stairs, not two minutes ago. You had best – '

'We'll see,' said Perrin. 'He intruded, you say?'

'He did, indeed,' cried Miss Ballew in ringing tones. It was
the very word.

'I'll see if we can pick him up,' said Pat Perrin, sounding
competent and unruffled. He hung up at once.

Miss Ballew rolled a bit and sat up. She propped herself
on the headboard. She was trembling. 'This really – ' she

gasped. 'I don't know when I've been – What did happen? How did he – ? Who – ?'

The girl, who had closed the door, came slowly around the bed and sat down on the other one. Her eyes were a trifle aslant and an odd blue. She clasped her hands in her lap. Unpainted nails. Dark, decent dress. Modest ankles, shabby shoes.

Miss Ballew read all these signs as she was bound to do. 'You poor thing,' she said. 'I don't know your name.'

'Nell.' Not Sonya. Not Toni. Plain Nell.

'I'm Eva Ballew,' said that lady warmly. 'I suppose you were under such strain. I thought your manner was odd.'

'You don't know,' said Nell Wanly, and Miss Ballew's heart fluttered alarmingly. 'Oh Miss Ballew, I just had to tell you those lies,' the poor thing said, pathetically. 'I couldn't help it. He was in there, and he said he'd listen, and if I dared . . .'

'Simply terrible!' murmured the teacher. 'However did he get in here?'

'Oh, he knocked, and of course I went to see who it was.' Nell twisted her hands. 'And then he just pushed me.'

'Didn't you scream?' It was Miss Ballew's conviction that a woman always screamed. It did not, at this time, cross her mind that there was any other procedure whatsoever.

'But he said . . . said he was a friend of the people's,' said Nell. 'I didn't know.'

'No, of course, you couldn't know. Tsk. Tsk. Do you think he had been drinking?'

'Oh, he was!' cried Nell. 'Look!' She seemed very young and lithe as she reached for the whisky bottle. The cheap dress twisted tight to her body. Miss Ballew felt a shiver, rather a delicious one, along her nerves. She gazed, horrified, at the bottle's emptiness.

'And then,' said Nell, 'Bunny – that's the little girl – she . . . she woke up.' Nell put her face in her hands. She dropped the bottle on the floor to do so. Miss Ballew's mind swirled. So odd. Poor thing, so upset, to do such a disorderly thing.

'Now, now,' she soothed. 'It's all over, now.' And then, fearfully, 'Isn't it? There wasn't? Nothing?'

Nell took her face out and shook her head vigorously. Her tawny yellow hair tossed.

'Well,' said Miss Ballew feebly. Her heart raced. She felt unwell.

'Anyhow,' said Nell moodily, 'he only tried to kiss me once. He just kept on drinking and drinking.'

'You should have screamed,' Miss Ballew said trance-like.

'But I was so scared, I didn't dare . . . And I thought maybe, when Bunny cried so loud, someone might notice.' The girl's eyes rolled.

Miss Ballew felt herself flushing guiltily.

'And she didn't really "almost fall",' said Nell with sudden passionate indignation, 'at all! He was mad. That's what it was. He thought I was trying to, you know, get somebody's attention out of the window like that, so he dragged her away.'

'Oh, dear . . .' Miss Ballew thought how wise one is never to believe too hastily in what one thinks one sees. Always, she noted, wait for the other side of the story. 'And when she began to scream so, later? Why was that, my dear?'

Nell looked wildly around her, threw herself face down, and her shoulders heaved, and soon her sobbing shook the bed.

'Now,' Miss Ballew struggled to reach over but she felt dizzy, herself, and she couldn't make it. 'Now,' she said, 'don't – ' She thought, Someone must soon come. She herself was really not in any condition to deal with this any further. It was shameful, but she felt as weak as a kitten. Just hearing about it. The poor girl must have had a violent psychic shock. In fact, Miss Ballew knew herself to be suffering the same thing, vicariously.

'She got scared and began to cry,' sobbed Nell. 'She just got scared. That's why she began to cry. But he was so mad. It made him wild. He said she had to stop that noise.' The head slipped, the face turned, the wet lashes lifted.

Miss Ballew lay against the headboard and her rather long countenance was whitening. 'Then, it was *he*, in her room?'

'You saw . . .' the girl challenged.

'Yes, I saw. But it was too dark. I couldn't clearly see. Oh, my dear, if he has harmed –

'Oh, he didn't *hurt* her.' Nell said and suddenly she sat up again. 'He just made her stop crying.' A little smile – pitiful, it might have been – worked on her face. 'And there wasn't anything I could do because he locked me in the closet . . .'

'Incredible.' The teacher's lips were stiff.

Nell looked solemnly at her. The room fell . . . as if all its emotion-laden air swirled, falling . . . to silence. 'You know,' she said, 'I think he was insane.'

Miss Ballew said, 'Is there – Could you? A glass of water? Or could you call, perhaps the house physician. I really am afraid I am having rather a reaction . . .' She closed her eyes.

Insanity was obviously the explanation. For things so wild and wanton, insanity was the definition, really.

In the dim bathroom of 807, on the cold floor, Eddie stirred. His right arm moved as one moves in sleep. He turned a little to his left side. Then he lay still.

CHAPTER 16

The hotel detective, Pat Perrin, put up the phone and crossed the lobby, moving quietly. He opened the door to the base of the tall rectangular tube where the fire stairs ran. He discounted, from long practice, ninety per cent of what he had just heard. But for the sake of the other ten per cent, he stood and listened. Any sound, he knew, would come booming down to him.

And so it did. Someone was on those bare stairs. His own ears informed him. So far, so much was confirmed. He waited, quietly. He wore a gun.

Jed realized the echoing clatter of his descent in this confined space. Nimbly, he brought himself up against a door, stopped the second or two it took to rearrange his own rhythm, tugged the door in upon himself, and stepped steadily out to the sixth-floor corridor.

As he crossed the carpet toward the elevators a man – only a man – joined him. Jed took care not to be caught looking to see whether the other was looking. The man pressed the down button and, superhumanly, Jed did not. He set his suitcase down, denying the need of his nervous hand to hang on to it. It occurred to him, freakishly, that he had left a blue tie and a good pair of socks, damn it. His jaw cracked and he deliberately let tension out of it. Without fidgeting, he watched the dial, as the other man was doing, as all elevator awaiters seem compelled to do. The hand was coming down.

Disinterested, strangers, they stepped on in silent sequence

107

as the elevator obeyed the call. And in silent sequence they stepped out, below. Jed, looking to neither side, walked to the desk. His gait deceived. His trunk and shoulders showed no effort, but his long legs drove hard against the floor and bore him more swiftly than they seemed to do.

He said, crisply, 'Checking out. Towers, 821.'

'Certainly, Mr Towers.'

'Mind making it quick?' Friendly and crisp but not too urgent. 'Just got hold of a cancellation. I can get out of here to-night if I make it down to the station.' Jed looked at the clock in the woodwork behind the man's head.

'Yes, sir.' The clerk did not seem to put on speed but Jed was aware that he did, in fact, waste no motion. He recognized the skill in it. He made himself stand still.

Pat Perrin knew when no feet rattled on the stairs. He caught a boy and posted him, here, near where the stairs came down, at a door to a narrow passage that was the back way out. He caught another to watch the entrance to the bar, for one could exit to the street through that dim corner room. He himself had a brief word with an elevator boy. Then his skilled eyes ran down every man in his sight. 'Tall, light suit.' He weaved among the chairs. He moved along the carpet.

'You figure,' Jed was asking pleasantly, 'about twenty-five minutes to Penn Station?'

'That's close, sir. Might do it. Here we are.' The clerk turned the reckoning around. He took an envelope from a box and presented this, too. Jed saw his name before him in a script he knew. A note from Lyn. Lyn Lesley. He stuffed it into his coat pocket. (No time for her now.) He took money out.

Perrin's eye checked Jed's tall figure in the grey suit. *Dark* hair, *no* freckles, *white* shirt. He walked on by, the eye skimming.

Jed put his wallet back, picked up his bag, surveyed the way ahead, the not-very-long distance to that revolving door and

108

out. He was as good as out, already. The clerk already counted him for gone. To turn back, to speak again was like contradicting the forward flow of time itself.

But Jed put his palm noiselessly on the blotter and the clerk looked up.

'You'd better,' said Jed, speaking slowly and soberly and emphatically to be understood and heeded in this, the first and only time he would say it, 'send someone to room 807, right away. Trouble. A kid's in trouble. 807 and 809. A little girl. If you know where Mr and Mrs Jones went, call them. It's their kid.'

He turned swiftly and went, in that same smooth, deceptive, very rapid gait, in the shortest line to the revolving door and through it without a check.

Then he stood in the air, in the open night, and he was out of it, and it was their kid, wasn't it?

Pat Perrin knew someone on those stairs had got off the stairs. So much was true. Whether he rode down or not was a question. Now, Perrin peered through to the street, saw tall, dark, and handsome, in the white shirt, harmlessly pausing to light a cigarette. He pushed through and crooked a finger to the doorman, said a word or two. He raked Jed's back with his glance, conscientiously, turned, looped on his own tracks, and went back through the lobby because the other exit would be the one a fugitive would like. He saw Milner at the desk lift a startled hand as if to beckon. He signalled with his own, Busy (no time for him now), and he walked on by.

Jed shook out his match. All right. So he'd established Towers had nerves of iron. And what now? Cab? Bus? Subway? To the airport? His thoughts were jumpy.

A cab swerved in to the kerb and braked in his very face. He thought it was querying him. Then he saw that it had a fare to discharge here. He stepped aside.

As the domelight went on, he could see her. Young woman, blonde, attractive, in party clothes.

He stood with his bag at his feet and blew smoke out. Here was a cab, emptying before him, becoming available, and in it he would be gone, like smoke. Smoke poured out of his mouth. He half turned his head. He looked (because he was in some way forced to look) up behind him at the chequered façade, the tall bulk, the flat and secretive face of the Hotel Majestic.

The girl from the cab, with her change, bills and all, in her bare hand, got out. She swept her long skirts, aquamarine velvet over rosy silk, up in one hand. Her golden slippers stepped quickly on the grey sidewalk. She went by Jed. Her gaze crossed over his face blankly, and he, blankly, watched her go by, for they were strangers.

Jed saw the doorman prance, and the door spin. The cab door, in front of him, remained open. It hinted, tempted, invited. Finally it said to him, 'Well?'

He moved nearer and put out a hand, ducked his head, brought his bag up in the other hand, and his knee up . . . Something hit him. It seemed to him that he was struck in the face by a barrier as soft, elastic, and yielding, as easy to pass through, as a cobweb. Something that was no more substantial than the air itself. Only a faint scent . . . breathing into his face from the cab's closed place. A perfume, it was, that stopped him, because he knew that scent and it made his stomach turn over. Why, he reeked of it, himself! Of course. It was *on him!* It came from himself.

He barked, 'Sorry,' and slammed the door. He lifted his hand, giving permission and command. Go ahead. The cab's gears snarled at him. It went away in a huff, saying with a flounce of its back bumper, 'Whyncha make up your mind, stupid!'

Jed trod his cigarette out. He felt rooted on the sidewalk and his feet kicked at the invisible chain. All right. He would not shut himself up with that sickening odour. That's all. He'd air himself free of it. Walk, then. Lug your damn bag. But get gone, stupid! He held hard for anger, this kind of anger. His hand came up to brush before his face.

Milner, the man at the desk, leaned over, full of summons, but Pat Perrin was out of range of a soft hail and a loud hail would never do. Milner's still-startled eyes blinked. Towers,

821. Eighth floor, sure enough. Fellow might know what he was talking about. Something wrong in 807? Peter O. Jones, 807 and 809. Mr Milner didn't know where the Joneses were. He was annoyed as well as startled. But of course he would check. It would never do not to check up on such a warning.

He took up a phone and pivoted, looking anxiously for some reason at the hands of the clock. 'Give me 807, Rochelle, will you?'

'Sure thing.' Rochelle alerted. She thought, 'Oh boy, something's up!' She thought, '*I* smelled a rat up there hours ago.' She was rather pleased. There were long stretches on this job that were pretty dull. She hoped this was going to be interesting. Whatever it was. She said softly, 'What goes on, Mr Milner?'

Since Mr Milner did not know, he was haughty. 'If you'll ring them, please?'

'O.K., O.K.' He heard Rochelle ring them. He stood, holding the phone, staring at the clock as if he could by the wilful power of the human eye stay the hand, as Ruth O. Jones went rustling by behind him.

No need to stop for her key, she reflected, since of course Nell was there to open the door. Besides, it would take time. Her feel of time wasting was because she'd been wishing too long to come. Only that. Why, the lobby was just the same, just the same.

Ruthie and the jitters. How Betty would laugh! Betty the city mouse. Betty the louse, who'd begged off. Although why on earth I assume *she's* so darned reliable . . . Betty and *her* system of values . . . Betty who doesn't even know, yet, what a woman's in the world for . . . It was the blood tie, of course. It was the mere fact that Peter's sister could not be a stranger.

Now Ruth began (for everything upstairs would be just the same) to pick and choose among excuses. One could not say, I came because I don't trust you an inch, my dear. No. But one could say, I came for a clean handkerchief, which would be pretty feeble. Obviously, no shoulder straps to break. Oh, say a pill, say some special remedy brought from home. For a headache, say. It would do.

There was a man in a brown suit talking in rather an official manner to the elevator boy. He kept on talking.

'I beg your pardon,' Ruth asked. 'Is this car going up?'

'In a minute, ma'am.'

'Thank you.' She stepped by.

They kept muttering together. The boy said, 'Never rode with me.'

Ruth's foot in the golden slipper twitched. Oh, don't be silly! Surely a minute doesn't matter! (Except on the inner clock of her apprehensive bones.)

CHAPTER 17

Nell let the water run. Then she filled the glass. She stood, holding the glass, and twisted the faucet once or twice, on and off. Her face was sullen and a little bored and weary, as she looked down at the form of the little man on the bathroom floor, lying as if he were normally asleep, twisted a bit to one side, as if to be comfortable.

The skin around his eyes twitched, as if the bright light affected him. She frowned faintly, and then her whole body seemed to shrug, to lift off the problem and let it go. The hell with it.

She snapped off the light, opened the door that she had so speedily put between her and room 807, and pulled it after her quite deftly as she stepped through. 'Miss Ballew?' She was all sweet service.

The schoolteacher, with her eyes closed, was silently reciting poetry. It was a trick to play on the release of the fearful substances to the blood, on the whole panicked interior chemistry. Sometimes, by taking the brain's attention elsewhere, she could wait out, slow down, and defeat the pound of the goaded heart.

'Oh, thank you, my dear. Really, this is so feeble of me.' Her teeth chattered. 'But I lead rather a quiet existence. I rarely . . .' The phone rang. The glass was still in Nell's hand. 'I'll get it,' chattered Miss Ballew and jerked around.

Nell sat down quietly. Her toes turned in, then out, almost imperceptibly. Her finger-tips danced a little on the cool damp glass.

113

'Yes?' quavered the teacher.

'This is the desk. I've had word of some trouble. Perhaps you can tell me?'

'Trouble!' burst Miss Ballew. 'Yes, *certainly*, there has been trouble. I spoke to *someone*, long ago! Now, who was that? Really, by this time you ought to have accomplished something. Do you mean to tell me! Didn't you *stop* him?'

'I beg your pardon,' said the astonished voice.

'Did you or did you not stop that man! I told you – I described him.'

'Who is this, please?'

'This is Miss Eva Ballew. I have 823 but I am now in 807 as you ought to know since you are speaking to me here. Now, I reported this trouble minutes ago – '

'Yes. Yes, I see, Miss Ballew,' he broke in. 'The house detective must have taken – '

'*Must* have! Are you guessing! Who are *you*, pray?'

'I'm at the desk, ma'am.'

'And do you mean to tell me that you do not know! See here. Is anything at all being done?'

'The house detective evidently – '

'Evidently! Are you men or mice down there? Where is *he*?'

'He is evid – He is looking – That is, I see, now.'

'You are too late and too slow,' she spoke on top of him, 'and it has been too long. You have irresponsibly allowed that ruffian to escape.'

Milner's spine curled. 'But is the child all right?' he demanded.

'The child? Why, yes, I believe – '

Milner, man, not mouse, was delighted to say, disagreeably, '*Do you mean to tell me that you do not know!*' and snap, 'Someone responsible will be up there at once,' and slam down the phone. But all the same, he was relieved. Pat Perrin knew about it.

Miss Ballew hung up and her eyes were pained. So often this physical weakness had betrayed her. So often it had led her to be ashamed. She knew so well what one ought to do, but the weak flesh was a drag.

114

'What was it?' Nell said.

'They . . . someone will be up. They seem confused.' And I, thought Miss Ballew, am a pitiful despicable cowering wretch. And she tried to shift her legs.

'He got away?'

'Evidently.' It was no use. Her legs were mush, still. 'My dear,' she said sadly, 'hadn't you better see to the child?'

'Oh, yes,' said Nell quickly. But she rose without haste, in fact, rather slowly and tentatively. 'Don't you want the drink of water?' She didn't seem to know what to do with it.

Miss Ballew received the glass. She was not a fool. Now, as she knew her guilt, and realized that someone ought long ago to have gone in to the poor frightened child, the terrified little girl, she began to wonder why Nell had not gone. Nell, whose responsibility she was, had fetched water for a stranger instead. It didn't ring right. First things had not come first. No, it rang wrong. Echoes of their first exchange began to come to her. Nell's rudeness and the odd manner. She could no longer so glibly excuse it. And she seemed, besides, to see in her mind's eye that the man in the corridor had no freckles on that averted cheek and no blue in his clothing.

She looked at Nell. She murmured, 'It's incredible, really.' The girl seemed to be waiting politely for her to go on and perhaps she didn't understand. 'It's hard to believe,' translated Miss Ballew. 'I've never heard such a wild story. There seems to be no sense . . . not even a mad method to this man's actions. Are you sure?'

'What?'

'Are you sure you didn't encourage him?'

'I haven't done anything,' Nell said, looking surprised. 'I don't know what you mean.'

This was an echo, too, and it rang false. 'Come now, of course you know what I mean.' Miss Ballew looked annoyed but she checked herself. 'Never mind. This is no time for debate. See to the child, my dear, and bring her in here, do. Poor, poor baby. When the detective arrives,' her voice faltered from its habitual tone of instruction, 'I daresay he . . .'

'He what?' Nell frowned faintly.

'I mean to say,' said Miss Ballew dryly, being fair, 'perhaps he's seen more of this sort of thing . . . perhaps more of it goes on than is dreamed of in my philosophy. And of course,' she added thoughtfully, 'the child . . . How old is the child?'

'How old?'

'She is not an infant? She is old enough to talk?'

'Of course,' said Nell wonderingly. 'She's nine, I think.'

'Then that is fortunate,' said Miss Ballew, 'for of course she will be able to corroborate your story.'

Nell was just standing there, looking stupid and even half falling asleep.

What a handicap to have so limited a vocabulary, thought the teacher. 'Corroborate means to confirm,' she explained, 'to tell the same story, or enough to prove it, do you see? That's why I point out – '

'And fortunate,' said Nell, 'means lucky.' She was smiling. Why, she was dancing! She stood on the same spot, there at the foot of the bed, but for a moment Miss Ballew had the distinct impression that she was dancing. Even her face had a twinkling, sparkling look. Impish, as if she'd thought of something, had an idea, or knew a mischievous secret. 'I know more words than you think I do,' said Nell. 'And I understand the future.' She flung up her hands . . . yes, it was a dance! (Miss Ballew looked on, bewildered.) And then the dark skirt flopped and fell out of the moving arc and reversed . . .

And the girl was leaning on her two stiff arms, her knuckles white on the footboard, her eyes very wide, very blue. 'I . . . I wonder . . .' The eyeballs turned in slow fear and the slow fear welled up in Miss Ballew.

'She's awfully quiet,' Nell said, softly, softly. '*Isn't* she?'

Miss Ballew clawed her own throat.

'Don't you think . . . it's funny?'

'F-fun – ' Miss Ballew wafted her arm across the air. Nell's teeth enfolded her lower lip. Now she looked very grave and thoughtful. She walked on soft toes to that inner door. Her hand was slow on the knob, and nerves in the teacher's temple turned excruciatingly with it.

The latch fell out. The door yawned. No sound emerged from 809.

'Bunny?' Nell called, softly, softly.

There was no answer.

'Bunny!' The girl's back shook as if with a long shiver. Only quiet answered her. Her eyes rolled as she looked over her shoulder. 'I'm afraid . . .' she whimpered.

Miss Ballew was afraid, too. She could *not* move. Her own ears knew that frightening silence was really there. 'But you said – But you told me he didn't . . . hurt . . .'

'He was in there, *afterward*. After you knocked. Do you think . . .'

'Don't think! Don't even say!'

But Nell's words fell like Fate. 'Maybe he remembered . . . she's old enough to talk. . . .'

'Our Father which art in heaven,' mumbled Miss Ballew. 'Beseech thee . . . from evil . . .'

'It would,' said Nell, glassy-eyed, 'be so easy. She's just . . . a little thing . . .'

'Go see!' screamed Miss Eva Ballew, up on her elbow but paralysed for all that. 'For the love of heaven, girl! Go *in* there and *see!*'

CHAPTER 18

Lyn touched his arm. He veered away from her touch as if he expected a blow to follow. (Yah! Iron nerves, Towers?)

'Lyn! Oh for – I thought . . .'

'Didn't they give you my note?'

She was there, and not an apparition, standing beside him and, in the light of the city night, her face was sweetly, soberly wondering why he was as startled as this to see her. Ah, she was sweet and sane!

'Gosh, you look . . .' He grabbed her woolly blue arm. 'What are you doing here at this hour? You been rattling around this town *alone!* It's too damn late, Lyn.'

'I'm not afraid. . . .'

'The street's no place . . .'

'I *haven't* been . . .'

'I don't care where you . . .'

'Nobody bothered . . .'

'You ought to know better!'

'Oh, don't be so . . .'

'Little fool . . .'

'Oh, Jed!' she wailed. They teetered back from the brink of the same quarrel. The same damn thing. Jed even stepped backward on the sidewalk.

'I guess this is where we came in,' he murmured.

'Where I walked out,' she laughed uncertainly. Her eyes were not merry. But they were sweet and sane.

He put his hand in his pocket. 'Jed, didn't you read it?'

'No, I . . . Not yet.' He fumbled for the envelope. He felt

118

troubled . . . troubled. Not ready to meet her. She was here too soon. He held her note passively in his hand.

'It's nothing.' She tried to take it, gently, but he refused to let it go. 'I've been waiting and waiting,' she said breathlessly. 'In the lobby, Jed. It was safe enough. I was just about to give up and go home. I went into the drugstore . . . saw you . . . I've been calling your room.'

He made no reply, no excuse, no explanation.

'I waited the longest time,' she said.

'Why, dear?' he asked gently.

Lyn's face looked as if she were touched to tears but she did not weep and she did not turn her face away. 'Because I'm sorry, Jed. That's about all there is to say about it. I'm ashamed to have been so stubborn and ornery. I'm sure you were more in the right than I was willing to admit while I was so mad.'

'Never mind.' He slipped his arm around her. 'Never mind. Never mind.' He thought, If this isn't like her! This kind of weird, high-minded, overdone fairness, this proud dragging down of her pride.

'I couldn't bear you to go all that way,' she said quietly, keeping her own balance, although he embraced her, 'and us mad. That's . . . all about it.'

'Was I mad at you?' he said, scarcely believing it.

'Where were you going?' She put her bare fingers to her eyes.

'Oh, I . . . was more or less lighting out,' he said vaguely. He felt very sad, very sad. He had a sensation in the breast as if the heart would break.

'Could we have one drink somewhere? And would you take me home? Will you make it up, Jed, and get the nasty taste out of our mouths, before you go?'

He looked down at her. 'You beat all,' he said gravely. 'But you're sweet. How come you do the way you . . . ?' He broke off. He looked up and the stone face on the building above him had no expression, nothing to say.

'I called you things I don't believe,' Lyn said in a low voice. 'Is it a date?'

Something bigger than he was took him and shook him

like a rat. He covered the shudder up by grabbing for his suitcase. 'It's a date, Lyn.' He let his mouth curve, his voice was as tender as it wished to be, and she smiled like the rainbow.

Jed looked away, off over her head. Why did he feel so troubled and sad? Here was she, stubborn little love, trying to get back where they'd been. And why not? So Towers had his date, after all. Didn't he? Right back where he'd been. Wasn't he? (Episode over. Close quotes. File and forget.) Here's Towers in the evening with his own girl under his arm and a honey she was, wearing that proud humility, *believing* (his heart sank because it was so heavy), trusting that he was going to match it. That they'd be together again. Be that as it may, the night was young and nothing was lost. Not a thing. Was it? And he could park the suitcase somewhere and on with the dance! March on! Te dum de dee . . .

Proceed, Towers. From where you were. Advance, right out along the line, the line you cut in your time, the track you see before and leave behind, that goes, if you are smart, straight without any stupid detours. . . .

'Please, Jed, let me have my note?' she begged softly. 'You don't need . . .'

He looked down. He said, 'No.' He put it back in his pocket. Oh-ho no! he thought. This we look into, in some dark bar, 'Just a minute, honey,' he went on, sounding to his surprise exactly as if this was what he'd planned to say from the moment she had touched his arm. It came out so smooth and easy. 'Something I want to check, a minute. In here.'

She smiled. It was all right with her. Anything he said, of course. He thought, What a reckless attitude *that* is! But he touched her and with tenderness pushed her into a slot in the door and pushed the door, following.

What the hell was he going back in for? Curiosity? One thing, he'd surely keep it from Lyn, what he was up to. It was nothing, anyhow. Take a minute. No need to invent a lie, for her . . . innocent, reckless little love! No, he'd just take a quick look around, that's all. He thought he could tell, pretty quickly, if they'd got up there to the little kid, all right. Surely repercussions would sift down to the lobby, which he would be able to feel. Maybe no other guest could notice, or catch on at all. But surely, he could tell. And rest his mind about it.

That would really close it off. Lyn would never ask. Or, she'd take it, if he gave no answer, if he never explained. There'd be nothing to mention, nothing even to think about, once he knew nothing was . . . dangling.

Towers could then proceed.

In itself, the hotel now knew something was up. The news ran on its nervous system, in the minds of its own people. The guests were unaware and might never become aware of this, as the guests had been unaware of many things on many other occasions. But the hotel knew now.

Rochelle sat at her board. She knew. She prepared to be the spider in the middle of the web. All things would eventually come to her.

Milner knew, and was nervous behind his front, although his front remained as wooden and polished as the walnut around him. He was about to leave his post. He'd had a quick word with the Assistant Manager and that one agreed that Milner himself must go up there. He would emerge from his inner place and take over at the desk.

The bartender knew, in his dim barricade in the far corner of the farthest corner. The porter, emptying ash trays, had a faint knowledgeable air. The bellboys knew. 'Some guy got away,' they dared say to each other softly, but they veiled their watching eyes.

Perrin was almost resigned to the idea that the man had got away. If he had not, but still lurked somewhere, where was it? No redhead and so forth in the corridors, in any of the public rooms. Not in the bar's deepest recesses, not in the men's rooms. If he was registered and had a room and lurked *there*, it might take a little doing.

Perrin strode up to the desk and caught Milner. 'Who we got that's tall, redheaded, freckle-faced, light suit, blue shirt?'

'Nobody,' said Milner. 'Say . . .'

They wiped trouble from all their faces. The Assistant

Manager said, 'Yes, Mr Hodges.' A guest took his key, made a firm didactic statement about the weather, went away.

'On the trouble in 807?' the manager said.

'Yeah, dame described this man . . .'

'Just what did he do?'

'Intruded,' said Perrin dryly.

Milner said, 'It was a man who tipped me. Is the kid all right?'

'Who?'

'Who told me? It was . . .'

'No, no. *What* kid?'

'Little girl. Jones.'

'I'd better get up there,' Perrin said thoughtfully. 'Nobody told me about a kid.'

'That's not good, having a kid in it. I was just going . . .'

The manager said, 'Uh – keep it quiet.'

Two of them swung off separately. Milner negotiated his way around the walnut embankments. Perrin met him again, near the elevators.

The elevators knew, although they whispered up and down without telling.

'Couldn't have hurt the kid,' Perrin remarked. 'All she said, he intruded.'

'All she said to me, did we stop him,' agreed Milner. 'Ran out, did he?'

'Yeah, he's not up there now.'

'Nerves?' said Milner hopefully. Perrin shrugged. Whatever it was, they assumed it was all over but, of course, the hysterics.

An elevator whispered down. 'Say, that's Towers now.' Milner peered. 'Fellow who tipped me. Thought he – oh . . .'

'Oh, what?'

'He's got the girl. She found him.' Milner relaxed.

'Eight,' said Perrin quietly and stepped on. The boy moved only an eyelash. But he knew.

'Up? Up?' carolled Mrs McMurdock. 'Come, Bobo. Come, darling. Time for beddy-bye.' The little dog ran into the elevator and sniffed moistly at Perrin's socks. Milner and he exchanged looks. The car started upward.

'He loooves to ride,' said Mrs McMurdock. 'Doesn't he, Bobo? Doesn't he, boy? Loves to ride! Yes, he does! Just loooves to ride!'

She did not know.

CHAPTER 19

Ruth, as she rode gently upward, stuffed her change into her little evening bag without looking down at her hands. She kept watching the blank metal door beyond which the floors were sliding by. She was the only passenger. The car made no stop but hers. As it sailed toward a soft landing and went into the little shuffle for the precise level of the eighth floor, she felt a perverse regret for the ending of an ordeal, a resistance to the necessity of shifting from one mood to another.

She stepped out. Behind her, the car stayed where it was a second longer than was normal while the boy listened to the quality of the silence up here. It seemed to be mere silence. Disappointed, he looked at his lights, yanked the lever, and sailed upward.

For Ruth, the corridor was just the same, just the same. She hurried to her left. She turned the corner.

The door of 807 looked just the same . . . as bland and blank as all the others. Prepare to shift. Inside, the girl would be dozing, and Bunny fast asleep, and the debris of her parents' dressing would be strewn about just as they had left it. Shift. The mood, now, is hushed. It's the mood of – All's well. Naturally. Of course it is. Ruth tapped gently.

At once, a much agitated female voice cried, 'Oh, yes! Come in! Oh, come in!'

Ruth's mood leaped like lightning. Her hand leaped to the knob. She burst into the room and met the frightened eyes of a stoutish middle-aged woman she'd never seen in her life before, who was half-sitting, half lying, in a strained position on Ruth's own bed. The woman's black dress was awry over her stout leg and her mouse-coloured hair was awry, too, 'Who are you!' cried this stranger in a voice that was also awry.

But Ruth put first things first.

Her gold bag fell out of her hand. Without a word, she flew, hands up, across 807 to 809. She batted the partially opened door and it swung wider. 809 was unlit. Ruth aimed herself like an arrow at the light switch. She flashed around.

She saw Bunny's two bare feet twitching on the bed and the girl's dark back bent. Ruth cried out, 'What's the matter?' She got one glimpse of Bunny's bound mouth, and then saw the girl's face blinking at her over the shoulder, the drowsy evil in the sullen careless glance, and she knew what the wicked hands were about to do.

Making no cry, Ruth simply flew at her. Her hands bit on the shoulders, and with all her might she heaved backward, to get the evil away. Still, she did not scream. Instead, she called out in almost a cheerful voice, 'It's all right, Bunny. It's me. It's Mommy.'

The shoulders rolled, writhed, and slipped away from her. The girl's body turned with vicious speed. Ruth felt herself knocked backward and the small of her back was wrenched as it slammed against the other bed and she felt her neck crack with the backward weight of her head. She flipped herself quickly over and slipped downward to her knees, hearing silk rip. She fastened both hands on an ankle. She crawled backward, yanking and pulling, out from the narrow place between the beds. *Get it away from Bunny*. This was first. And Nell came, hopping, tottering, kicking . . . and her hands clawed for Ruth's face, hurting Ruth's eyes.

O.K., thought Ruth. *All right*.

Ruth had not always been a gracious young matron, a pretty wife, a gentle mother. In her day, she'd climbed many a tough tree and hung by knobby knees off ladders with pigtails dragging. And she'd chased the other kids off rafts and over rooftops. And she'd played basketball, too, on a touch team, even in so-called free style, which meant she had pulled hair and bitten and gouged with the rest. And she'd run up and down the playing fields of many schools and been banged in the shins by hockey sticks. She'd had her bruises and given them. The world of direct physical conflict, violent and painful, had not always been beyond her ken.

'So!' she hissed with her teeth closed. There was lightning on her eyeballs as she got her hands in that yellowish hair and yanked, and the girl screeched and fell forward, twisting, and Ruth rolled on the hard floor to get from under her.

She felt the teeth in her forearm and pain as claws ripped at her cheek. Ruth's long rosy nails went into the other's flesh, where she could, and with the sharp spurs of her heels she slashed at the other's shins. Her own head thudded on the carpet and hands like wires sank in her throat.

She wouldn't have screamed, anyhow.

She pulled up her knee. Silk ripped, velvet tore. She put her sharp golden heel in the wildcat's stomach and straightened her leg and Nell went sprawling. Ruth walked on her knees and dived on her, got the hair, whammed the head to the floor.

But the head bounced. The body in the dark dress was taut and strong. It wasn't going to be that easy.

Ruth heard herself growl in her gullet, now it was free. Fast as the fighting went, she yet summoned with a cold brain old strengths, old tricks, and when they were not enough, she began to invent . . . She had realized, long ago, that she fought, here, something wild and vicious, that wanted to hurt, that didn't care how. Probably mad, and strong by that perfect ruthlessness.

But Ruth, too, was fortified. She was wilder than the tomboy she used to be. She was more vicious than the girl athlete. She was Bunny's mother and she was easily able to be absolutely ruthless in that holy cause.

She said to herself, *O.K. All right*. And she was not afraid.

It never crossed her mind to scream. It seemed her sole and simple duty and even her pleasure to fight with all her body's strength and her mind's cunning. (Outside of any rules, if that was the way it was, and O.K., too.) It did not cross her mind to wonder who would win, either. She sank her own strong teeth in the enemy's wrist, while she tried with her mind to think just how she was going to conquer . . . what trick would do it . . . even as she was tossed and the merciless elbow was crushing her breast.

Miss Ballew managed to get her feet to the floor but her weight would not balance over them. The column of her leg would not stand, the knee joint would not lock. She knew now she would be forever haunted by remorse and shame if she did not force herself to help in this emergency. But she was not well. Her heart hurt. There was a sharp pain in her side. Her mind knew that her body was lying, and her heart pitied the body's treasonable victory, as her lips prayed cravenly for someone else to come.

CHAPTER 20

The moment he was inside the lobby, Jed knew that the hotel, in itself, was aroused. The alarm was spread. He saw it in the stiff pose of a different head behind the desk. He knew, too, that there had been, and yet was, a search going on. He saw that in the veiled turn of all the eyes, in the porter's spine. Looking for someone? For whom? For *him*, no doubt.

It came to him that he was taking a certain risk in the mere act of stepping back within these walls. Sure, they were looking. Once more his mind played back its recorded impressions, a glimpse of the fellow in the brown suit weaving among the chairs, and his beckoning hand and the doorman's response, and the doorman's *belated* prance to his normal duties. The man in the brown suit had been looking for someone, all right. For whom, if not for Jed?

All the way across the lobby, he could see that very suit, the same man, over there right now, waiting for an elevator. The clerk to whom Jed had given warning was beside him, and all the way across the lobby, Jed knew when they spoke his name.

What was this?

They were *looking* for him and they, for some reason, were not looking for *him*. He saw himself split in two, the object of their search, and merely Towers who had just checked out of 821. They hadn't put it together yet. They would, sooner or later. And easily. For instance, right over there lounged the boy-who-had-brought-up-the-ice. Who was, all by

128

himself, the missing link. When would his hunting eye catch sight of Jed and recognize?

Jed guided Lyn so that she stood with her back to the elevators and he, bent as if to listen to her, could watch them with an eye-beam over her head. Those two men were authority. Obviously. Were they *only now* going up to see what was wrong on the eighth floor? If so, they were darned late! Wires must have got crossed. It had been a long time.

(A long, long time for a helpless, frightened little girl to wait in the dark for her daddy or his equivalent.)

He ground his teeth. What was going on? Lyn stood obediently, her head thrown back to look up into his face. She didn't know why they were standing here. She trusted there was a good reason.

He said, rapidly, 'Do you mind? I just want to see . . . Talk to me. Make some remarks, hm?'

'You're being mighty mysterious,' Lyn said lightly. It was so plain she trusted he had good reason. 'Mine not to wonder why. Me and the six hundred. Lyn, number six hundred and one.'

He felt his jaw crack. 'Keep talking.'

The elevator took on its passengers . . . two men, one woman, and a scampering little dog.

'Nothing is quite so numbing as to be told to say something. Makes your mind a blank. Just like on long distance. Hm . . . I like raspberry pie very much but the seeds do get in my teeth. I'm very fond of cucumber sandwiches in the summertime. Is this better than the weather? Am I doing all right?'

'You're fine.'

Jed was farsighted, been so all his life. He could see from here the indicator moving on the dial. He could not read the numbers but then he knew already where the eight came. He said bitterly, 'Why in Christ's name didn't I lock the damn door!'

'If I ask questions,' said Lyn placidly, 'I won't be making remarks, will I? Cross out "will I".'

'The door *between*,' he growled. What he was telling he didn't know.

'Oh, between. Well, that's nice. That's quite illuminating.'
'If I had any brains . . .'

'Oh, you have, Jed. I think you have. Good-looking as you are, you must have a brain. I think it's very possible. Lessee, what's my favourite flower? At a time like this, I ought to know so I could tell you. But I like too many kinds, too much. But you take roses.'

Although he kept his eye on that dial, he knew Lyn's face was full of peace. She had no right! His glance flicked down. She had her hands in the big pockets of her coat and her back was bent in a sweet, almost yearning arch, in order for her face to turn up to him, and her eyes were sweet and sane and full of peace because she believed . . . She was a little fool to believe in anybody!

'You look about nine years old,' said Jed with a whipsnap of anger. And he sent his eyes again to the dial.

'Oh, I don't think so. I think I probably look about nineteen and just as if I've got a terrible crush on you, a bobby-socks-type crush. And you look like thunder, Jed. If I knew what the matter was I'd try to help. But you know that, of course.' (I even trust you to trust me.) 'Mine only to keep talking, eh? Why, then, I'll go ahead. Babble. Babble. Do you care for the chamber music? No, that's a question. Well, I always say it depends. And it does. Everything depends . . .'

The hand on the dial had stopped . . . must be at about four. It seemed to be stuck there. Was it out of order?

'Come, boy. Come, boy. Ah, naughty Bobo! (Loves to ride!) But this is home, boy. Home! Now, Bobo must be a good boy. Biscuit? Bobo want his biscuit? If Bobo wants his biscuit . . . Oh, what a naughty, bad doggy! Bobo! Listen to me! No . . . more . . . ride. Do you understand, sir? Beddy-bye, now. Come, Bobo.'

Bobo retreated to the inner corner of the elevator and sat down.

Mrs McMurdock giggled in her throat. 'So ki-yute! Isn't that – Little monkey! Bobo, boy, Mama will leave you. Biscuit, biscuit?'

The hotel's people stood silent. Mrs McMurdock was a

guest. Bobo was a guest. A guest need not know all there is to know. They wore small chilly smiles, not too impatient, not too amused, either.

Bobo frisked between Milner's ankles.

'Shall I pick him up, madam?' the elevator boy said most respectfully.

'No, no. Now, he must learn,' said Mrs McMurdock. 'Now, he'll mind in a minute.' The trouble was, Bobo did look as if he would mind, any minute.

The hotel's people cleared their throats with professional patience. It wasn't going to be very pleasant placating that woman on the eighth floor, admitting to her that her wicked intruder had got away.

In the lobby, Jimmy said, 'Hey, kids, sumpin's funny! See that fellow over there, one with the girl? Say, what was the room again?'

'Room 807.'

'Yeah,' drawled Jimmy. 'Yeah . . .'

Jed's eyes flicked in his stony face.

' . . . partial to rum,' Lyn said, 'with pink stuff in it. And you sure can get thirsty, talking so much. Filibuster is running down, Jed. Don't elect me senator, anybody. Is it all right now? Can we go?'

In Jed's head exploded the loud NO for an answer.

Her face changed. One second, sweet and pretty, and pleased with the nonsense she was able to spin. The next it had lost all that pretty animation, light, and colour. Jed did it. By the look he bent on her, he wiped the pretty peace off her face.

He said, quietly, 'I'm a rat, Lyn. A complete rat. Go home.'

'But Jed, I've been wait – '

'Don't wait any more. Never wait for me.'

He stepped around his suitcase. His face was flinty. His muscles surged. He went across the lobby in a walk so smooth and fast that he seemed to float.

He knew that bellhop straightened with a start.

To hell with that!

131

He pushed on the door to the fire stairs.

Ah, God, NO!

He shouldn't have run out on that little kid! What kind of rat did such a thing? A rat like Towers. A complete no-good . . . He was sad, he'd been sad over it a long time. So sad his heart was heavy.

Ah, NO!

A pair of socks wasn't all he had left and lost up on the eighth floor. And left, forever. Gone, like smoke! Yeah. You can't catch it back again, no more than you can a wisp of smoke. Thing like that, you can't retrieve.

And who would know? *Towers* would know.

This trip, all the way down to the lobby and out, wasn't even as good as a detour. There wasn't a way back from this side road to the main track. No way *on* again, *in* again. Rat forever, amen.

But he went up. Went up with all the great strength of his long powerful legs, three steps at once, then two, but pulling on the rail, around and around climbing the building more like a monkey than a man going upstairs.

Passed the buck. Towers! Let the old lady take care of it. Towers! White! He sobbed breath in.

He thought, I don't know what I'm doing . . . know what I did . . . Never even thought to lock that door. Could have made sure to keep her out of there. Could have done that much. He and he *alone* (not Eddie. Eddie was out on the bathroom floor) . . . Towers *alone* knew what kind of sitter that Nell turned out to be. Knew the poor little kid was waiting. The old biddy couldn't know *that*, and where was she all this while? Arguing? No reason to think . . .

No, no. What Towers *alone* knew was that, reason or no reason, there would always and forever be some risk with that Nell around. But a risk for somebody else, of course. For somebody else's kid. A little thing who couldn't do a thing about it. So *Towers* figured the risk to his own six feet three, to his man's hide, to his . . . what?

Now, he couldn't remember any risk for Towers. For *nothing*, he ran out. For the sick shadow of nothing at all, he'd lost what he'd lost.

This complete revulsion was making him sick. O.K. Cut it out, Towers. What's done is done. Take it from here.

Eighth floor?

He must be in pretty good condition.

Yeah, condition!

There was the elevator. And there they stood, talking. Questions and answers, with the elevator boy. The hell with them. They didn't know there was a risk. Or they'd hurry. He couldn't understand why they hadn't hurried. Jed rushed past.

Aw, probably Bunny was all right. Probably. Pray so, and if so, here's Towers heading right back into the middle of this jam, for nothing. Doing no good. But maybe not for nothing. He didn't know. All he knew was, while he could still move for himself, he was going to make sure. He was going to bust in there and if the old biddy hadn't found her yet, Towers was going to untie the little kid and the hell with everything else . . . and five seconds more, one second, one pulse beat more was too long.

Room 807's door was wide open. The old biddy, crouched on the edge of the bed, took one look at Jed's wild figure and heaved in her breath and let out a scream to wake the dead!

But Jed was in 809 before it died.

Nell, hair hanging over her eyes, had one knee on either side of the slim body of a woman, supine on the floor. Their hands were braced, hand against wrist, arms against aching arms. The woman on the floor had blood on her mouth and her cheek was torn and her breathing was shallow and diffi-cult. But her eyes were intelligent and they yet watched for her chance.

Jed took little Nell by the short hair of her head. He ripped her away. She came up in his grasp, screeching, and hung from his hand, limp in surprise like a sawdust doll.

In the corridor, Milner and Perrin saw the racing figure and in their startled ears rang the woman's scream. Perrin got his gun in his hand as they began to run.

The door of 807 was wide.

'The man,' croaked Miss Ballew, voice thick and hoarse.

'That's the man!' Oh, she knew him. By the indescribable. By the habits of motion, the line of the back, the tip of the shoulder, the cock of the head.

'The *one*,' she sobbed. 'The man . . . the same one!'

Perrin looked toward 809.

He saw a tall man with a face of utter fury drag, by the hair of her head, a small blonde girl through that door. Saw him drag her around the wooden frame as if he didn't care whether she lived or died, as if he didn't care if he broke her bones.

'Drop that girl! Let her go!'

Jed's head went back and the eyes glittered down the long straight nose. 'The hell I will! You don't – '

Perrin fired.

CHAPTER 21

Ruth O. Jones lifted her shoulders from the carpet, and pulled her twisted rags and tatters aside to free her legs. She wiped the blood off her mouth with her arm. She combed her fingers through her hair. Some of it, torn out at the roots, came away in her broken nails.

She walked on her knees – there was no need to rise higher – over to Bunny's bed.

She paid not the slightest attention to the gunshot as it blasted off, behind her.

She said, in her firm contralto, 'O.K., honey bun? For goodness' sake, what happened to *you*?' Her cut mouth kissed the temple lightly. Her fingers were strong and sure on those wicked knots.

Jed kept standing, somehow, because he had to keep an eye steady on Nell. She fell on the floor when he had to drop her as if she had been a sack of meal. As soon as he was sure she lay as limp as she seemed to lie, he looked at his right hand. He took it away from his left side and looked at the bright blood on it.

He looked at the men, standing tense and threatening in his path, and he tried to smile. The elevator boy was behind them. Then he saw his girl, Lyn, behind *him* . . . looking, as if she peered through trees in a glade, between the men's bodies, in at the strange tableau.

Ah, the little fool! 'Go home,' he said.

Then he heard it. In the other room, Bunny began to cry.

Over Jed's face passed a look of peace and thanksgiving.

He turned, reeling, because he was wounded and no kidding, stumbled, and made for the big maroon chair. He thought he sat down in it. Perhaps it was more like falling.

'Oh, Jed!'

'But that's Towers . . .'

'It's the same man . . .'

Now, he was three. Or maybe only one, again. Or nothing. No matter. There was a difference in the way a kid cried. Funny . . . could you write down the difference in musical terms, he wondered. Pitch or timing or what? One kind of crying that gnawed on your nerves and pierced your head. This kind didn't do that. No, it didn't do that at all. It was a thing not unmusical to hear. . . .

Perrin, kneeling over Nell, barked, 'What did you do to this girl?'

Jed didn't feel like bothering to say.

Miss Ballew let out another yelp of pure shock. Eyes starting from her head, she reacted to her sight of the little man in the hotel's livery who was standing in the bathroom door, holding his head, looking out mouse-like at them all.

'Munro!' thundered Milner. 'What — '

Eddie blinked. Silence rustled down, that they might hear his feeble voice. 'I guess . . . Nell musta got into more mischief. Did she? My niece? Nell?'

'Who?'

Jed pulled himself from the mists. 'Nell, the baby-sitter. On the floor.' He braced himself, watchfully. 'Nutty as a fruitcake,' he said.

But Nell only rolled, drowsily. Her arm fell aside in sleepy grace, revealing her face. Her eyes were closed. The blue gone, her small face was left perfectly serene. There was a long scratch from eye corner to jaw. It looked as if it had been painted there, as if she felt no pain. She seemed to be asleep.

'That's Nell. Yes, she . . .' Eddie tottered to look. 'That's the way she did — before,' he said in awe. 'After the fire, they say, she slept . . . just like that.' He swallowed and looked around at all their set faces. 'How can she sleep?' he whimpered.

'Somebody,' said Jed wearily, 'go see. I suppose it's Mrs Jones. This one pretty near killed her.'

Perrin got off his haunches and lurched through the door. Milner's horrified eye sent fury in sudden understanding where, from his point of view, it belonged. 'Munro!'

'I . . . didn't think . . .' said Eddie. 'I kinda kept hoping she'd be all right. But I guess . . .'

'Next time, don't guess,' said Jed. 'Lyn, go home.'

'Not now.' She moved toward him, drawn. 'I won't, Jed. I've got to know . . .'

He closed his eyes.

When a fresh scream rose up, out there in the other room in another world, Ruth's finger-tips did not leave off stroking into shape the little mouth that the wicked gag had left so queer and crooked. 'That's right. Just you cry. Golly, Bun, did you see me fighting! Wait till we tell Daddy . . . missed the whole thing . . .' Ruth held the little head warmly against her battered body. There was comfort soaking through from skin to skin. 'Cry it all out, sweetheart. Cry.'

'Mrs Jones?' a man said to her. His hair seemed to her to be trying to stand on end.

'Go away. Hush. Please call my husband . . .'

She stroked and murmured on. Not until she heard Peter's voice did her wounds and gashes remember pain.

'We're just fine,' Ruth said quickly. 'Jeepers, have we had an adventure!'

Peter's face was dead white as he looked upon his wife and child.

'She was the crossest sitter I ever saw,' Bunny said indignantly. Her arms went around her daddy's dark head where he had hidden his face against her. 'She tied my mouth all up, Daddy, so I couldn't cry. She certainly didn't want me to cry awful bad.'

Peter roused and looked at those stockings.

'Bound and gagged,' Ruth said quietly. Her face said more.

'G-gosh, she must have had terrible ears.' Peter's voice trembled. 'I expect she's got sick ears, Bunny.'

His hands curled and uncurled. Ruth's eyes said, I know. But it's over. Be careful.

For Bunny didn't realize what had almost happened to her and it was better if she didn't. You mustn't scare a little girl who's nine so that all her life she carries the scar. You must try to heal what scar there is. Ruth knew, and deeply trembled to know it, that some day she would leave Bunny again. And with a sitter, of course. She must. (Although not for a good while with a stranger. Maybe never again with a total stranger.) Still, they would go gaily as might be on in time and they would not permit themselves to be cowed, to be daunted. They dared not.

Poor Peter, shaken and suffering, right now, and fighting so hard not to betray it. Peter knew all this as well as she. They were tuned to each other. 'Bunny's fine and I feel fine, too,' she told him. 'Really. A few scratches. Did they take her away?'

They're coming. They'll take her to a hospital,' added Peter, for Bunny's sake, 'because she's sick, really. She doesn't know how to get along with people who are well.'

'Will she get better,' said Bunny with a huge snuffle, 'from those sick ears?'

'I don't know, pudding. They won't let her be with well people any more, unless she gets all better.'

Bunny's shuddering sobs were becoming like the soft far murmur of the last thunder of a departing storm.

'Daddy.'

'What, Bun?'

Ruth felt the head turn on her breast. 'Did you have fun?'

Peter couldn't answer. But Ruth could. 'Oh, Bunny, it was lots of fun. And Daddy made a good speech. I wish you'd been big enough to go.' She rushed on. 'Daddy stood up and all the people, everybody was dressed up . . .'

Peter looked upon the condition of his wife's clothing. 'Those . . . scratches, hon,' he said in a minute, sounding as if half his throat was closed. 'There's a doctor out there.'

So the doctor came in and looked them both over.

'You know,' said Ruth when he had gone, licking the antiseptic in her mouth, 'I pretty near had her licked! I think!' She laughed. 'I must look terrible but I feel fine.'

And she did. Ah, poor Peter, with the retrospective horror

and the wrath locked in and buttoned down. But Ruth had got rid of it by tooth and claw. And she remembered, now, with relish, certain digs and blows. She felt quite peaceful. Fulfilled, she thought, the tigress in me. 'Hand me in some of my things, Peter. I'm going to bed in here with Bun.'

'O.K., girls.'

'Maybe we'll order hot chocolate! Shall we? Let's!'

'In the middle of the night!' squealed Bunny and the sweet smooth skin of her face rippled in the warning of delight to come.

Peter O. Jones, with a smile covering (from all but his wife) the tears bleeding out of his heart, went back to 807.

CHAPTER 22

Eddie was gone, damned for a reckless fool, with all the anxious ignorant hope he'd called his caution dust in his whimpering throat. (Don't worry, Eddie, Marie would say.)

Milner was gone, to harmonize with the walnut, downstairs. (Keep it out of the papers, if we possibly can.)

Perrin was gone. ('Sorry, Towers. You can see how it was?' 'Sure. That's O.K.') He went with Nell.

And Nell was gone. Still seeming asleep, looking innocent and fair. Only Jed spoke to her. Jed said (and it seemed necessary – somewhere once, this he had planned to say), 'So long, Nell.'

She was asleep so she didn't reply. Yet there was a lazy lift of the lashes. (They won't do anything to me.)

Nearly everyone was gone. Miss Ballew remained, sick in her soul, with the doctor's suggested sedative in her hand. Jed was in the big chair again, bloody shirt loose over the vast bandage. Lyn was still there.

The doctor warned once more that Jed must take a few days' rest before trying to travel with that wound. Then, he was gone.

'You'll stay over, Jed, won't you?' Lyn's mouth was stiff.

'A couple of days, at least. I'll see.' Jed's side was stinging like the devil, now. Telegrams, he thought, but time for that later. Maybe he'd break his cross-country trip and stop to see the family. Felt like it, somehow. Worry them, though, if he turned up shot. 'Lyn, will you please . . . Your family's probably . . . Why don't you go home?'

'I will, soon.' She didn't look at him. She looked at her trembling hands.

Peter took Ruth's things to her, came back flipped up his tails, sat down, put his head in his hands. 'Jesus.'

Lyn said, with that stiff mouth, 'You're terribly upset, of course. Shouldn't we go, Jed? If I can help you to your own room . . .'

'Or I,' said Miss Ballew drearily.

'Don't go. Ruth wants to say good night. A minute.'

'Your little, uh, Bunny's all right?' asked Jed.

'Soon be. Kids bounce back. Thank God. Drink with me?'

Jed didn't feel sure. He felt this room rejected him. But he was *fallen* in this chair.

'I ought to go home,' said Lyn whitely. 'I don't mean to hang around . . . be in the way.'

'I ought to go,' said Miss Ballew. (To be a worthless old coward and on top of that be fooled and fail in the mind, too!) 'I was of very little use.'

'Take it easy,' Peter said. 'Better try and take it easy, all of us.'

Jed shifted his stiff side, reached slowly for the pocket of his coat, for the envelope. He managed to open it with one hand. It said, 'Dear Jed:' And that was all. No more.

Well. He looked back into dim reaches of time. It would have been enough. It would have been plenty. He crushed it up and put it back in his pocket. He didn't look at Lyn.

Peter passed drinks. 'Nonsense, Miss Ballew. You need this. There.' He sat down. His brown eyes locked with Jed's grey. 'As I understand it, you left Bunny tied up? But you told them at the desk on your way out?' Peter's voice was light, tentative.

'I figured it wasn't my business,' said Jed levelly. 'I didn't want to get into a mess. I figured to get away.'

Well, he hadn't got away. He'd got shot. And Towers was a rat. So, then, he was. The little girl was O.K. now. Mother, too. Nothing, thank God, they couldn't get over. So . . . if

Towers was left in his rathood, that was not too important to them, any more.

Grey eyes locked on brown. 'That's the kind of rat I am, I guess,' Jed said quietly. 'Later, I got a little nervous . . . a little too much later.'

Miss Ballew's lips trembled. 'I was so stupid,' she said. 'I was worse than no use. My *fault* . . .'

Jed's grey eyes met hers. They said, Don't blame yourself too much. They said, I understand. They said, Us sinners —

'Seems to me,' Jed drawled, 'if you're hunting for blame . . . if I hadn't come over here in the first place . . .'

'If I hadn't walked out,' Lyn said bleakly.

'No. Lyn . . .'

'You think *I'm* not doing any iffing?' Peter asked. Brown eyes met grey. 'If I'd even looked at the girl with half my brain on it. Me and my big important speech! I left it to Ruthie. Of course, she got it. In her bones, the way she sometimes does. If . . .'

Jed shook his head.

'Ruth knew I needed her. She chose. Even *Ruth* can if . . .' Brown eyes said to grey, *All us sinners*.

Peter got up to pace. 'Ruth says she had her licked. But I don't know . . .'

'I don't know, either sir. I couldn't say.' Eyes locked again. 'Now, don't kid me, sir,' Jed said gently. 'They weren't two steps behind me. They'd have been on time.'

And then he smiled. Because it only mattered to Towers, now, and Towers could take it. 'Tell you, it isn't often a man says to himself, You ought to be shot, and right away, someone obliges.' He moved and made the wound hurt. It was not so bad. It was like a session with the hairbrush, or a trip to the woodshed. He didn't mind.

But then Lyn said, as if she broke, 'I'm afraid.' Why, she was all to pieces. She wasn't *Lyn*. She looked white and old and sick and she was shaking to pieces. 'I'm scared to go home. That's the truth,' she wailed. 'I'm scared of the night. I'd go but I'm afraid. Such t-terrible things . . . I don't know anything. I'm scared of what a f-fool I've been.' She wept.

Jed winced. 'And you ought to be,' he said grimly. But it wasn't *Lyn*. It was sick and ugly.

Ruth said, 'Ssssh . . .' She stepped out of Bunny's room, leaving the door wide. She wore a man's woollen robe because she was cold, now, with shock. (And Jed was glad, remembering Nell in the long silk.) But her battered face was serene.

Lyn choked off her whimpering.

Peter held Ruth's hand to his cheek. 'Asleep?' he whispered and she nodded. She looked lovely, this little blonde Mrs Jones.

'Drink, darling?'

'Not on top of chocolate.'

'Ruthie, would you be scared if I took this young lady home?'

'Why, no,' Ruth said, smiling.

'Uh, you see, Towers can't do it. He ought to be in bed.'

Jed said, appalled, 'Yes, and I'm going there. But listen, get the hotel to send somebody. Lyn can't go alone. But you can't leave Mrs Jones, sir.' She's had enough! he thought.

Ruth smiled at them all. 'Don't be afraid,' she said, gently.

'Here we sit, with our hair turning white,' murmured Peter, in a moment, but his eyes were shining. ' "Don't be afraid," she says.'

'Well, you *dasn't!*' Ruth smiled. 'Or what would become of us all?'

She wasn't long for them. She wasn't all in room 807. She kissed Peter's brow, made her good nights. She didn't say thanks. Perhaps she forgot, or she knew . . . She withdrew, went back to her sleeping baby, and the door closed behind her.

They sat, sipped quietly. Lyn's face was pink, her eyes were ashamed, her back was straighter. Jed thought, I know her. I know what she's made of. And, he realized, *she* knew more about Towers, the real Towers, than anyone else on earth. Something grew, here . . . never could have grown had they gone, say, to a show. Something known, for better, for worse. He touched her hand. She turned hers and her icy fingers clung. 'Put an ending on my letter, sometime, honey?'

'How, Jed?'

'The regular ending,' he said, soberly. Yours truly. That was the way to end a letter.

Lyn smiled like the rainbow.

I'll just have to take care of her, he thought. She mustn't be afraid. His fingers moved, humbly, on the soft back of her hand.

Peter said, 'Yep. We oughta be scared, all right. Ignorant optimism won't do it. Won't do it. But we've got *not* to be scared, just the same.'

'Courage,' sighed Miss Ballew. She rose to say good night.

'We are strangers,' Peter said darkly. 'Whom do we know? One – if you're lucky. Not many more. Looks like we've got to learn how we can trust each other. How we can tell . . . How we can dare . . . Everything rests on trust between strangers. Everything else is a house of cards.'

Miss Ballew went around to her room, having been drinking at midnight with strangers! Strangers and friends! She was, and not from liquor, a little bit intoxicated. She felt warm around the heart and a bit weepy and quite brave.

Peter came back and sat down, gazed at the two of them, moving his lips. 'Damn it,' cried Peter O. Jones. 'I wish I'd said that!'

'Said what, Mr Jones?'

'What I just said!' Peter was cross.

Lyn's eyes met Jed's and dared be a little merry. 'But . . . Mr Jones, you just *did*. Didn't you?'

'In my speech!' cried Peter. '*Now*, I have to think of a better ending.' He glared at them.

Pandora Women Crime Writers

For further information about Pandora Press
books, please write to the Mailing List Dept. at
Pandora Press, 11 New Fetter Lane, London
EC4P 4EE

THE HOURS BEFORE DAWN
by Celia Fremlin

Behind the curtains of Britain's 1950's suburbia,
a harassed mother is at the end of her tether.
Louise Henderson's kids cry, scream and shout
ceaselessly. Her husband whinges and wants
his dinner on the table, his shirts ironed.
But it's not the suburban mediocrity of her life
that horrifies Louise. There's something about
the lodger she has taken in that terrifies her.
Louise knows she's seen this woman before,
but she can't think where.

Pandora Women Crime Writers
May: LC8: 190pp
Paperback: 0–86358–269–9: £3.95

EASY PREY
by Josephine Bell

Well known to aficionados of crime fiction,
Josephine Bell, author of *The Port of London
Murders*, has created another riveting web of
intrigue and death.
When Reg and Mavis Holmes advertise for a
lodger they get the wonderful Miss Trubb who
seems kind and gentle and ready to help with
their young baby. But Reg and Mavis soon
learn that they've entrusted their 6 month old
daughter to the protection of a convicted child
killer . . .

Pandora Women Crime Writers
May: LC8: 254pp
Paperback: 0–86358–271–0: £3.95

SOMETHING SHADY
by Sarah Dreher

Stoner McTavish, lovable amateur detective
embarks on another adventure in the company
of her girlfriend, Gwen.
A woman has disappeared from her workplace,
a huge shabby country house turned mental
hospital known as Shady Acres. Desperate to
find out what has happened to the woman,
Stoner poses as a mental patient at Shady
Acres . . . with terrifying results.
This is the second in the Stoner McTavish series
by American author Sarah Dreher.

Pandora Women Crime Writers
May: LC8: 264pp
Paperback: 0–86358–241–9: £3.95

MISCHIEF
by Charlotte Armstrong

Made into the film starring Marilyn Monroe, this
Charlotte Armstrong novel is a brilliant
portrayal of one tense night in a New York hotel
room.
When newspaper editor Peter O. Jones and his
wife Ruth are staying in New York for a night
out they seem quite happy to leave their little
daughter alone with her babysitter in their
plush hotel room.
But for their child it's the start of a night never
to be forgotten, a night that could scar a child
for life, if that life is allowed to continue.

Pandora Women Crime Writers
May: LC8: 190pp
Paperback: 0–86358–272–9

LONDON PARTICULAR
by Christianne Brand

A car crawls through fog-bound London. Its
passengers, a middle-aged doctor and his
anxious female friend, are responding to a call
from a dying man. But this man was not dying
from any sort of illness, it seems more like
murder!
Christianna Brand, author of *Green For Danger*,
has produced another brilliant atmospheric
tale set in a smog-bound London.

Pandora Women Crime Writers
May: LC8: 254pp
Paperback: 0–86358–273–7: £3.95